MARTHA MAY MCKENZIE

AND
THE MAGIC CAKE
BIG MISTAKE!

BRIAN STARR

ARCHWAY
PUBLISHING

Archway Publishing books may be ordered through booksellers or by contacting:

Archway Publishing
1663 Liberty Drive
Bloomington, IN 47403
www.archwaypublishing.com
844-669-3957

Because of the dynamic nature of the Internet, any web addresses or
links contained in this book may have changed since publication and
may no longer be valid. The views expressed in this work are solely those
of the author and do not necessarily reflect the views of the publisher,
and the publisher hereby disclaims any responsibility for them.

Any people depicted in stock imagery provided by Getty Images are
models, and such images are being used for illustrative purposes only.
Certain stock imagery © Getty Images.

Interior Image Credit: Brian Starr

ISBN: 978-1-6657-3781-4 (sc)
ISBN: 978-1-6657-3779-1 (hc)
ISBN: 978-1-6657-3780-7 (e)

Library of Congress Control Number: 2023901600

Print information available on the last page.

Archway Publishing rev. date: 11/08/2023

For my little witch—
whose imagination and wonder amaze me daily.

CONTENTS

CHAPTER ONE
MARTHA MAY MCKENZIE

Martha was at it again, baking up mischief as usual. "A pinch of magic *here*—and a tiny pinch *there*," she said with a focused eye, raising her hands high and shaking them like salt and pepper shakers as she sprinkled her magic. When she was finished, after the last sprinkle fell, she closed her eyes and chanted softly.

"Slimy, green, warts and a hop. You're in for a surprise with this lollipop."

She then opened her eyes, smirking and exceptionally pleased with herself after adding the final touches to a fresh batch of her homemade, double coated in magic and dusted with sugar, *special* lollipops. Now, all that was left for her to do was to hide those lollipops in her favorite hiding spot until she was ready to use them and open her shop for business. *Here we go again*, she thought as she poured herself a fresh cup of coffee to jumpstart the morning. After adding a few packets of sugar (seventeen packets, to be precise), a cap full of witchnip, and one creamer, she was now ready to sit back and wait for her first customer of the morning. As long as she had her coffee, nothing could go wrong. But she wouldn't be able to enjoy that coffee, *not a single sip,* because her first customer happened to be nearby.

A young boy was walking the sidewalks of the Square with his grandmother. As his feet hit the cobblestone with excitement, his grandmother shuffled her steps swiftly beside him, trying to keep up. He held her hand in his with a big smile, dragging her along as they visited the locally owned shops.

The Square was always alive with visitors from all over— townsfolk and tourists alike—who equally enjoyed the nostalgic little shopping area. But no one was more excited than the young boy. He absolutely loved when his parents took him for a weekend visit to Texas to see Grandma. Every time he visited, she'd take him to his favorite shop, the Tasty Treat, where you were guaranteed a toothache! It was one of the oldest shops in town and one of the most popular.

Mr. Ferguson was the owner and operator of this deliciously delectable shop, always dressed to impress in his trademark red suede vest, puffy red-and-white-striped shirt, and red silk tie. The Tasty Treat had been in his family for generations, but Mr. Ferguson wasn't only a simple, well-dressed shop owner; he was a *master* at his trade. He never sold anything without tasting it first. Over the years, that meant *a lot of tasting,* which meant *a lot of cavities.* Poor

Mr. Ferguson only had one tooth left, but this didn't stop visitors. His shop was always full!

Mr. Ferguson was known for having the yummiest, lip-smacking, tongue-tantalizing, belly-busting treats for miles, with a little bit of everything to satisfy anyone with a sweet tooth. He carried old-fashioned candy, new-fashioned candy, and combined the two, forming re-fashioned candy. He had lollipops, jawbreakers, and homemade fudge. He also handmade the best flavors of ice cream—like bubble gum rainbow swirl with marshmallows and chocolate peanut butter hunky chunky avalanche. He made some gross ones too—like spicy liver and onions, and pickled pistachio farts. And though they sound awfully disgusting, he somehow made them tempting and sweet.

He had every assortment of chocolate you could imagine— milk chocolate, dark chocolate, white chocolate, smooth chocolate, chunky chocolate, powdered chocolate to make liquid chocolate, chocolate *dipped* in chocolate, and even his own creation of chocolate, which some said was suspiciously *too* chocolaty. There were jars on every shelf, filled with licorice ropes, soda caps, candy rocks, twirled taffy, and peppermint twists. He even sold minibags of pure, raw, crystalized sugar—for those who needed a quick fix. The list went on and on. His best-seller, though, was something called a booger blaster—a small, colorful, chewy candy no bigger than a jelly bean. It was said to be so good that it made your boogers taste sweet, hence the name. Secretly, the booger blaster was all the leftover unsold candy in the shop, mushed and squished into small balls and sold cheap. Mr. Ferguson *never* let any of his sweets go to waste.

Surprisingly, the Tasty Treat wasn't the shop that caught the young boy's eye today. Instead, he spotted a new shop next to it— one he had never seen before and one that made all the other shops seem to disappear. He was drawn to it. It wasn't anything like the other shops in the Square; it was more like an eerie hut, one that looked centuries old. But this hut was like no other. It wasn't like a hut at all. It was much taller, like three huts stacked into one, and it was built very strong. Unlike all the other shops made of wood, this shop was made entirely of stone, all kinds too—big stones, little stones, and lots of itty-bitty tiny stones, like pebbles and rocks. On the very top was a heavy stack of thick yellow straw for a roof. The

inside couldn't be seen because there were no windows, only a single wooden door. But this was a *massive* door, as tall and wide as the shop itself, or so it appeared.

Although this shop was much taller than the other shops and stood in broad daylight, it somehow remained hidden in a shadow, untouched by the sun. It was spine-chillingly unnatural. And for some strange reason, it was the only shop surrounded by pestering crows. There were bunches of them! They hovered about, circling the shop. Perhaps it was the crows who cast the shadow. *Caw, caw.* Their screechy squawks sounded like nails scratching against a chalkboard, sending shivers down the young boy's spine. *Caw, caw.* It was a bit creepy, but it piqued his interest. He had been looking forward to filling his pockets with candy, but now he wanted to know what was inside this new shop.

"Grandma, what shop is *that?*" he asked, pointing ahead.

"I don't quite know," she answered. She let go of his hand. "How about you go take a look inside."

"Are you sure, Grandma?" he asked nervously.

"Of course," she assured him with a granny smile as she scooted him with her wrinkly old hands. "Go on now."

The young boy took another look at the shop. He didn't think it was a good idea to go in alone. He turned to his grandmother to ask her to join him, *but she was gone. Gulp!*

"Grandma?" he whispered.

He turned in a circle, searching everywhere, but she was nowhere to be found. It was as if his grandmother had vanished into the busy passing crowd in the blink of an eye. So he mustered up some courage and walked over to the shop alone. As he approached, he noticed a piece of paper nailed to the door with a

gigantic, rusty, bent iron nail. On that paper, written with blotchy black ink, was each and every single letter from the alphabet, all scrambled and scattered about. Some of the letters were written more than once, some more than twice, and some more than that. He didn't know what to make of it. Then …

The letters suddenly moved—all on their own—as if they were alive!

The young boy shook his head in disbelief. *No way that just happened!* he thought, looking down at the paper. He'd never seen anything like it before. He blinked twice and assured himself he had imagined it, but this was not his imagination. The letters were *indeed* moving. They slowly came together, one by one, forming a sentence:

Welcome to The Witch's Brew.

Wow! the young boy thought, wide-eyed and surprised. *Could there really be a witch in there?* He reached toward the door handle but cautiously hesitated. For just then, the door mysteriously creaked open, just slightly enough for a fog to seep through the tiny crack. It danced around his face as an intoxicating aroma filled his nostrils. He took a huge whiff, breathing in the delightful smell, and exhaled with a pleasant sigh. *Ahhhhh.*

Now he *had* to know what was inside! He was too curious not to. So he placed his little hands on the massive door, one hand on the handle and the other in between the cracked space, and slowly opened it the rest of the way, straining as he gripped and pulled with all his might.

The young boy was both nervous and excited as he entered the shop. To his surprise, the inside was astonishingly smaller than expected, unbelievably so! It wasn't as tall as it appeared outside, and the door wasn't as big anymore, either. It was as if the entire shop had shrunk as soon as he'd walked in.

Dozens of flickering candles lined the stone wall and lit up the inside. There were thick climbing vines everywhere, sprouting from the ground and reaching all the way to the ceiling. From the corner of his eye, it seemed like the vines were moving. He slowly extended his arm and touched them to ensure they weren't. As he did so, he realized how odd and uneven the ground felt beneath him, forgetting about the vines completely. He then lifted his foot and noticed the entire floor was dirt. *How strange,* he thought as he lowered his foot back down.

He peered off to the side and saw a wonky, handcrafted broom leaning to his right. It looked like it had been carved using a dull potato peeler. It was by far the oddest-looking broom he had ever seen. *Why would anyone have a worthless broom like that?* he thought. *And for a dirt floor?* But he didn't focus on it too much. His curiosity was all over the place.

Looking around, he noticed a few wooden tables. They were large and round and looked like huge spools of thread—without the thread. On each table was one or more freshly brewed pots of coffee. The pots looked old and antique, and no two were the same. And what the young boy had thought to be fog was, he discovered, nothing more than the steam coming from these pots. Oddly, however, there were no chairs at any of the tables. And where were the cups? Also, there didn't seem to be any electricity inside. So how were these pots kept hot and steamy without being plugged in?

This shop was indeed different, and it smelled amazing. But in the end, it was only a coffee shop, and the young boy had no interest in coffee. He'd seen enough. Now it was time for him to visit the Tasty Treat, fill his pockets with as much candy as possible, and find Grandma.

But before he could turn to leave, a gust of wind from out of nowhere swooped in, slammed the door shut, and blew out all the candles—all but one.

Suddenly, an old lady draped in rags stepped forward!

She towered over the young boy as he quivered in her shadow, gripped with fear. At first, he was unable to see her face in the dimly lit room. But then, this faceless woman reached above him and grabbed an unlit candle from the wall, placing the wick next to the still-lit candle and then setting it back. As she did so, all the other candles lit back up at once! Now he could see her face—and he could see it clearly.

Aside from the thick, hand-sewn black eye patch, this old lady wore over her right eye; she wasn't scary looking at all. He felt a bit foolish for his cowardice.

"Don't be afraid," the old lady said, ironically speaking in a low and spooky tone.

"I'm not afraid," the young boy assured her, bravely puffing out his chest.

"Not yet, you're not."

Gulp. The young boy looked up at the old lady, who was looking down at him with a mischievous smile as if she had been expecting him. He stared into her one mesmerizing, fantastically blue eye, unable to look away as she pressed her lips together and stared back. She was like a giant to him, standing tall with poise. Her skin was old but fair and smooth, not as wrinkled as his grandmother's, though she seemed about the same age. She was rather lovely-looking, but her clothes were horrid. She dressed like a wandering fortune teller, completely covered in drabby, patchy old rags with different colors and fabrics. Her rags hid her feet and dragged the ground when she walked. She wore tattered and frayed fingerless gloves, a green glove on her right hand, and a blue glove on her left. Only her fingertips showed. But they were nothing like the condition of her gloves. They were pristine, manicured, and polished to perfection. What wasn't covered by her hand-sewn rags or mismatched gloves was hidden beneath her hair.

This old lady had an outrageously wild mountain of untamed hair, the likes of which belonged in a zoo, with never-ending locks of beautiful golden-brown curls that fell to the floor. To the young boy's surprise, there wasn't a single white strand. But it was a whopping mess, like a thick, heavy blanket, untidy and never made, though it appeared soft and silky. Every now and then, he'd catch a glimpse of her shiny, shimmering silver earrings. They were shaped like crescent moons with dangling stars that softly clinked and chimed each time she moved her head. The sound was enchanting, and it echoed through the entire shop. But what stood out most to the young boy were the shriveled, dried-up macaroni noodles on a string the old lady wore proudly around her neck. They looked *disgusting* and much older than she did.

"You must be Billy," the old lady said.

"How do you know my name?"

She stood there with her finger on her chin, still staring down at him. "I know many things," she replied.

"Like what?" he asked nervously.

The old lady answered his question *with a question* as she began to circle him slowly. "Do you believe in magic?" She dragged her finger along his shoulder.

Billy began to speak.

But she cut him off before he could answer. "That's a rhetorical question." Then, once she was behind him, she leaned in close.

He felt her warm breath on the nape of his neck.

"Magic is real!" she shouted, clapping loudly.

Billy jumped, startled by her sudden outburst. He trembled as goose pimples raced down both arms, leaving him looking like a freshly plucked hen.

The old lady patted him on the back and chuckled. "I won't bite," she assured him. "Sorry for the theatrics. Please come in. Magic *is* real, but it didn't bring you here today. Your grandmother did."

Billy sighed with relief. "How'd you know that?"

"I already told you," she replied. "I know many things."

"Like what?" he asked a second time.

"Well," she said, rubbing her chin. "I know you like candy."

Billy rolled his eyes. "Every kid likes candy."

"Ahhh, correct," the old lady agreed. "But some kids like it too much. Take me, for example. When I was your age, I ate candy all the time." She popped her dentures from her mouth, quickly sucking them back in and slurping up the dribble that followed.

"*Ugh!*" Billy grunted in disgust. "That's gross!"

"Ahhh, super gross," the old lady agreed once more. "But that's what happens when you like candy too much—and you don't eat your vegetables."

"Vegetables are stupid," he declared. "I never eat my vegetables. I hate them."

"I know," she said. "That's why your grandmother brought you here today. She asked me to help her with her naughty little grandson, who refuses to eat his vegetables. *All* the grandmothers around here bring me their naughty little grandchildren."

Billy's stomach sank. "Nuh-uh," he stammered nervously.

"Oh yes," the old lady assured him, tilting her head. Then, amazingly, her arms seemed to disappear as she reached deep into her curly locks.

Billy wondered what she was doing, fiddling with her hands in her hair the way she was. But to his delight, she pulled out a green lollipop shaped like a frog.

"Wow!" he said." How'd you do that?"

"Magic, of course," she replied, handing him the lollipop. "From one candy lover to another."

"For me? Thanks!" he said excitedly. Billy didn't care for one second that this lollipop was unwrapped or that it had come from her hair. He quickly jammed it into his mouth with bliss and chomped it to bits within seconds.

13

Chomp!   Chomp!   Chomp!

Without realizing it, he had eaten the lollipop *and the stick!* He clearly had a problem when it came to candy.

"So why am I really here?" Billy asked, scraping the roof of his mouth with his tongue. "If you were going to try to get me to eat my vegetables, you wouldn't have given me candy just now."

"You're absolutely right. What an astute observation," the old lady said. "But that was no ordinary candy. That candy will help you to *want* to eat your vegetables."

"I'll *never* eat my vegetables!" he shouted. "I wish I didn't have teeth! Then I wouldn't have to eat *any* vegetables!"

"Careful what you wish for," she mumbled, shaking her finger at him.

"Who are you, anyway?" he asked. "My Grandma's never mentioned you before."

"*Well*, where are my manners?" she said. "Allow me to introduce myself." The old lady jumped on the tips of her toes and twirled in an awkward dance as she shouted her introduction. "I am Martha May McKenzie, mother of one, grandmother of two, and owner of this fine establishment! I also recently acquired a goat. But above all that—**I'm a Witch!**"

Billy couldn't believe his ears! *There's no way she's a witch,* he thought. *No way!*

He needed to be sure he'd heard correctly. "A witch?" he asked, intrigued but doubtful.

"That's right," Martha confirmed. "But a good witch."

"That's impossible," he declared. *"You can't be a witch."*

"Why do you say that?"

"Well—where's your black cat?" he asked, looking in a circle with his arms in the air. "You can't be a witch without a black cat."

She immediately took offense. *"Black cat?"* she repeated, folding her arms.

"Yes!" he said with confidence. *"Witches have black cats.* You only have coffee. You're a barista at best."

"That's stereotyping," she said, unfolding her arms and shaking her finger at him again. "And I won't have it! Don't be a nincompoop. So what if I don't have a black cat? That proves nothing!"

"Well, still," he pressed on. "You don't look like a witch. Where's your pointy hat? Your warts? Your boils? Your skin isn't even green *or* slimy."

"Oh yeah?" she questioned, with her elbows out and her knuckles pressed on her hips. "And exactly how many witches have you met? Please. Do tell."

"Well, none," he replied, looking down, shuffling his feet, and then quickly looking back up. "But in movies, witches are ugly and gross and smell bad too!"

"Not this witch!" She raised her elbow high and took a great big whiff while wafting her hand toward her armpit. She leaned over and offered him a whiff too.

"Ugh, no!" he said as he crinkled his nose and backed away.

"I smell fabulous," she sang. She smiled and fluttered her eyelashes. "Only bad witches emit an odor. Believe me. You will know for certain when a bad witch is nearby. A foul odor of rot and dog vomit follows them wherever they go. They smell as gross and off-putting as papaya."

Billy still didn't believe her, and he had no idea what *papaya* was. He continued to question Martha with doubt. "Well, why are you wearing an eye patch then?" he asked. "Witches don't wear eye patches. Only pirates wear eye patches."

"*Really?*" she huffed, lowering her hands and slumping her shoulders. "OK. How many pirates have you met?"

He knew better than to fall into her trap and answer that question.

"Smart boy," she said with a grin. "I'll tell you precisely why I wear an eye patch. Better yet, I'll show you."

Martha placed her thumb under the rim of her patch and slowly lifted it. Billy cringed, anticipating the grotesque hideousness of what was about to be revealed, but he couldn't look away. He had to see!

She quickly lifted the patch the rest of the way.

"*Ahhhhh!*" he squealed like a frightened piggy as he covered his eyes with both hands. *Wait—that can't be right,* he thought.

He slowly lowered his hands and opened one eye. Then he opened his other eye. There was absolutely nothing wrong with Martha's eye. It was exactly the same as her other blue eye, and it, too, looked fantastic. He was disappointed but secretly relieved. *Thank goodness,* he thought.

"What'd you expect?" she asked. "A glass eyeball?"

"*Uh yeah!* But your eyes are normal," he pointed out. "So what's with the patch?"

"Well," she said, flapping her patch back down, "I just like it." She scooted her patch to the other eye, and they both giggled.

"It also helps me stay focused on good magic," she added, "and block out the bad."

"Bad magic?" he questioned.

But before Martha could answer, Billy's stomach made a funny gurgling sound.

"I don't feel so well," he said, grabbing his belly. His face quickly turned green. "I think I'm going to be sick."

"Well," Martha said. "That's because you, my friend, are about to become a frog."

"A frog?" he asked.

"That's correct," she replied. "A slimy, green, wart-riddled belly hopper."

"But how?" He moaned in pain.

"The lollipop," she reminded him. "I put a spell on it." She pulled a pocket watch from her hair and counted down the seconds. "You should become a frog in ...three ...two ...one."

But nothing happened.

Billy's stomach pain disappeared as quickly as it came, and he was no longer green in the face. He reacted boldly too. "That's some magic," he said sarcastically. "Ha!"

"Ha yourself!" Martha smiled. She dangled the pocket watch before him. "This old thing runs slow. You should actually become a frog ...right ...about ...now!"

But still, nothing happened.

"I knew you weren't really a witch," Billy said. He continued to ridicule Martha with sarcasm and laughter—until he realized that she was almost one hundred feet taller than him (measured in froggy feet, that is)!

Billy had, in fact, turned into a frog—warts and all! And he didn't even realize it at first!

Billy was speechless. He stumbled and bumbled and hopped right out of his clothes with his bulging froggy eyes opened wide. Everything looked enormous.

Martha scooped him up with a swift grab. Being this small was quite a change for Billy. Every movement in her hand felt like a wild ride on a roller coaster. He panted in fear as she brought him close to her face. She sounded like a loud giant. Each word she spoke pounded on his froggy eardrums.

"Hey, you wished for *no teeth*," she said sarcastically. "Well, *now you're all tongue!*"

Billy's slimy froggy arms and legs dangled in Martha's hand, and his slimy froggy body shook up and down as she chuckled.

"Don't be afraid," she said, flaring her giant nostrils.

Each breath felt like a windstorm to Billy—a *hot and stinky* windstorm.

"I meant it when I said I was a good witch."

She pulled Billy in closer and stared at him with her big blue eye, which was *not* mesmerizing this time. Because of his size—now—her eye was terrifying!

"So I offer you this deal. If you promise to take it easy on the sweets and eat more vegetables, *especially when your grandmother asks you to,* I'll change you back into a boy."

"I promise!" Billy croaked desperately. His throat bubbled out with each croak. "I'll do whatever you say! Just turn me back! Please!"

"Okie dokie," she said. She placed him back on the floor. "But before I change you back, I need to know that you are telling me the truth."

"I am telling the truth!" he croaked. "I swear!"

"Then prove it," she said.

"How?" he croaked.

She reached into her hair and pulled out a weeks-old, dried-up dead grasshopper she'd been saving for this very moment. "Eat this."

She placed the grasshopper before him. "This is a truth bug," she told him. "If you are telling me the truth, you will immediately change back into a boy after you swallow every last bit. But if you are lying, you will remain a frog—forever!"

Billy spat out his long slimy tongue without hesitation and snatched the grasshopper. He closed his eyes tightly, gobbled it up, and swallowed it down. He could feel its brittle body crumble and tickle his throat as it traveled down. Though he was a frog, he still had human taste buds, and this truth bug tasted disgusting! But it was all worth it in the end. When he opened his eyes, he was no longer a frog. He must have been telling the truth. However, he was now—*completely naked!* But he didn't care one bit about that. He was only glad to be a boy again; all he wanted now was to get as far away from this crazy old witch as possible!

He ran out of her shop without a second thought as fast as he could, screaming wildly the entire way.

Martha pointed her perfectly-manicured-and-polished-to-perfection finger and, with an explosive bolt of sparkling magic, zapped Billy's clothes—*bringing them to life.* They hopped up from the floor, took his form, and ran out of the shop, chasing after him. She couldn't let the poor kid run around naked—*that would be bad for business.*

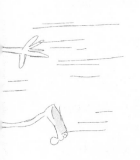

"Another satisfied customer." She smiled as she went to shut the door behind both Billy *and* his clothes. Even though he was only a frog for a few seconds, hopefully, this was a good lesson learned, and he'd never have to visit her shop again.

Afterward, she looked at the time on her pocket watch and gasped. "Oh, cinnamon sticks!" she said as she tossed the watch back into her hair. "I need to hurry!"

She grabbed her wonky broom and got ready to ride, the way witches do. But instead, she closed her eyes tightly, *thought* about where she wanted to go, and simply plucked a single bristle from the broom. *Pluck.*

Poof! Martha magically disappeared in a yellow puff of smoke.

You see, traveling witches had always been known to mount their brooms, using them to fly swiftly through the lonely night sky when all were asleep so as not to be seen. In the witch world, it was tradition. But not in Martha's world. She wanted to use her broom, day or night, whenever she felt like it. So she took it upon herself to shake things up a bit and used her magic to alter her broom entirely, thus creating a new and first-class way to travel—one that was remarkably colorful too. Though it wasn't traditional, it was far quicker and much more comfortable on an old witch's heinie.

CHAPTER TWO
SPARKLY MARTHA

Poof!

With another puff of smoke (this time green), Martha magically reappeared, having traveled all the way from her coffee shop to the front steps of her porch. And it only took seconds to do so, traveling by *bristle* instead of *broom*. *Zip zap zoom*, and she was there. After waving away the little bit of leftover green smoke still clouding her face, she adjusted her eye patch and leaned her wonky broom against the house, before walking inside. Normally, she wouldn't dare let her broom out of her sight, but she was frazzled, *razzled-frazzled*, and not thinking straight! She was expecting guests in precisely one hour and had much to do before they arrived. Her house was a mess, an absolute pigsty! She hadn't cleaned it in weeks (too many grandmothers with naughty grandchildren), so she needed to act fast. But it was way too much to do all by herself. She was going to need help—but not just any help. She was going to need *magical* help. Thankfully, she already had a helper for moments like this.

Throughout time, witches have always called upon helpers—be it a creepy crow, a slithering snake, or even a regular black house cat—to handle the small day-by-day tasks. Some witches even took extreme measures, such as a gargoyle or troll, when choosing a helper. No matter who or what a witch chose, they all shared a connection with their helper. These helpers even possessed certain powers of their own, but theirs were only simple powers, mostly used to do a witch's bidding. But Martha was allergic to black cats, *all cats, in fact,* and she didn't care too much for crows or snakes. And to find a gargoyle or troll, she'd have to go hunting for one. Ordinarily, for such an unordinary situation, they could be found far below the surface of the ocean, where the water boils black, hidden deep inside the belly of a bloodthirsty sea monster—*or sometimes,* but not always, they could be found beneath the very ground you walk upon, burrowed deep within a cold, dark, hidden cavern.

The thought of doing all that work, though, was simply too much for Martha. She hated caves and wasn't a big water person either. "Who needs the hassle?" she'd say. No. She used her magic and created a much more unique helper, one that came from within herself, one with a similar personality and sass.

Martha needed some of that assistance at this very moment, so she summoned her cheeky helper, but not in the manner you might think. Instead, she called upon her in the most unconventional, funny but nasty, you-wouldn't-believe-it way—*from her nose!* First, she pressed her finger to the side of her nose and closed one nostril completely. Then, she took a deep breath and, with a witch's force, blew her nose like a horn into the air. *Woosh!* Boogers and snot went flying everywhere.

But that wasn't all that came out.

A swirling bundle of colorful sparkles exploded from her nose in a magical whirlwind!

With all the colors of the rainbow, this giant snot cloud of sparkles swooped and swayed as they hovered over Martha, slowly piecing together each vibrant sparkle by sparkle. And once they were all pieced together, they magically sprang to life, shifting into the shape of a person—but not just any person.

They became none other than Martha May McKenzie, a sparkling version of the witch herself, known as Sparkly Martha!

Martha had summoned Sparkly Martha before, *many* times before. She was able to command Sparkly Martha with only a look, and with that look, Sparkly Martha would do her bidding. For example, if Martha wanted Sparkly Martha to help her conjure a spell over a boiling cauldron, then one look was all it took, and Sparkly Martha would do just that. But that was not what Martha wanted. She didn't even own a cauldron. Right now, all Martha wanted, more than anything, was to have Sparkly Martha clean her house.

So, Sparkly Martha did exactly what she had been summoned to do. She magically flew through each room of the house like a swirling tornado of sparkling glitter. She swept and mopped every nook and cranny and dusted all the shelves until they were exquisitely clean—spick-and-span! She removed the cobwebs from the corners, pulled the clumpy dust hanging from the ceiling, and emptied the stinky garbage piled high and bursting from the trash can. She even used her sparkling body to wipe the tub and then dived directly into the toilet. *Bloop!* She cleaned that poop flusher so well you could see your own reflection in the porcelain—and eat off of it too.

Afterward, she tossed herself into the washing machine and ran herself through a quick cycle—with *extra* detergent—while also tackling the dirty laundry. She then quickly dried her sparkles in the dryer, along with all the clean clothes, until everything, including herself, was fluffy and fresh. But her work wasn't done. She still had to match and put away at least a week's worth of Martha's socks and scrub the dirty dishes stacked tall in the kitchen sink—*which she did*. She went above and beyond and gave it her all, the works! She did, in a short time, what would have taken Martha all day to do—possibly all week. The house was clean, sparkly clean, just as Martha wanted.

Sparkly Martha, however, no matter how much she obeyed or how happy she looked while doing it, absolutely hated cleaning! It was boring, time-consuming, grunt labor, and it was never ever her mess to clean in the first place. Nevertheless, she always seemed to be the one left with the duty of cleaning up after Martha, a *messy, messy witch*, and she thought it was a waste of her magical talents. She hated *every time* Martha summoned her, mainly because it always involved some sort of grueling chore. Sparkly Martha was beginning to think Martha was plum lazy.

But Sparkly Martha *especially* hated being summoned for one reason above all—she hated being blown out of that old witch's nose like a useless booger. It was embarrassing! Why did she have to be summoned so? Why couldn't Martha keep her in a fancy bottle or a nice cookie jar? That way, she'd at least be covered in cookie crumbs instead of nose crumbs. To Sparkly Martha, it seemed cruel to be called upon in such a manner. Because of this, and their similar personalities, the two never saw eye to eye, and they bickered constantly.

Now, Sparkly Martha lacked the physical ability to speak using words. Though she possessed many other fascinating abilities, vocals had never been bestowed upon her. Perhaps that was intentional, so she wouldn't be able to argue with Martha. But that didn't stop Sparkly Martha from communicating. Martha always knew what she was thinking through her body language. And once Sparkly Martha was done cleaning, she used her body language and acknowledged herself with a proud nod. However, she also wanted Martha to acknowledge her as well and demanded a thank you.

But Martha was too busy eating a red banana she'd randomly pulled from her hair to notice. And after finishing her mid-morning snack, she carelessly threw the banana peel on Sparkly Martha's clean floor without a second thought. How rude! And worse, *Martha told Sparkly Martha to pick it up!* After all that cleaning?

"Throw that away for me," she said. "And return to my nose at once. *Chop chop!*"

Sparkly Martha didn't take this well at all. Her anger was bubbling beneath her sparkles. She huffed and puffed with her arms folded, marching back and forth, all while stomping her sparkly feet in a fit. *Stomp! Stomp! Stomp!*

"Don't be so dramatic." Martha scoffed. "It's just a banana peel."

But Sparkly Martha disagreed. It was much more than that. And even though Sparkly Martha was made of magic, and Martha could wield that magic, over time, Sparkly Martha had developed a relatively strong personality of her own, which made her a lot tougher to control.

Aside from being angry, Sparkly Martha felt unappreciated. She refused to pick up that banana peel. But again, it wasn't just the banana peel that upset her. She was simply tired of being a helper, an overworked and unpaid one at that. So she turned her back to Martha and did something very unexpected—she tooted a giant sparkly cloud. *Toot!*

Unlike most farts, *especially the really bad kind,* this one didn't linger or cloud the air or burn Martha's eyes like an onion or even stink, for that matter. There was no odor whatsoever. It was quite possibly the prettiest and sparkliest fart Martha had ever seen. But it was still a fart, which Martha thought was rude. *Gasp!* "How dare you!" Martha said. "I told you to pick up this banana peel and get back in my nose. Do what I said *or else.*" She picked up the banana peel herself and tossed it at Sparkly Martha, smacking her in her sparkly face (accidentally, of course).

But Sparkly Martha wasn't going back inside that nasty nose. Accident or no accident—**this meant war.** Sparkly Martha planted her feet firmly, confirming she wasn't budging. She picked up the banana peel and threw it back at Martha, this time hitting *her* in the face (not an accident).

Now Martha was furious.

"You're nothing but glorified dust!" she shouted. "Now you'd better get back in my nose before I turn you into a bowl of oatmeal and eat you—right now! I already have a spoon." She quickly pulled a spoon from her hair and showed it to Sparkly Martha, letting her know she was not bluffing. She then put the spoon back and lifted her head. She hooked her nostril with her finger and opened it wide, waiting for Sparkly Martha to obey.

But her threat had no effect. Sparkly Martha turned and glared at Martha with glittery defiance.

And with that glare, Martha knew exactly which devious action Sparkly Martha was planning to take next—because she had done it before, *many times*. A look of worry washed over Martha's face, and panic set in. She quickly pulled her finger out of her nose.

"Don't do it," she begged.

But Sparkly Martha slowly nodded up and down with a snide smirk as if to say, "Oh yeah. I'm doing it, you old kook."

She then squatted low and braced herself firmly with her sparkly fists gripped tightly. She opened her mouth *monstrously* wide, wider than her whole body, and sucked in air like a vacuum. *Swooooooooooo*. She sucked in as much air as she possibly could and *continued* sucking. *Swooooooooooo*. She didn't stop. Not once! *Swoooooooooooooooooooooo*. Her bright, sparkling colors soon faded as she swelled herself full of air. Like a dull beached whale in the heat, she continued swelling and swelling and swelling until …

Pop! Sparkly Martha burst!

She went from sparkles to sand, scattering *all over the place* in a single explosive second. Martha jumped from side to side, trying to dodge the sand. She hated loose sand more than anything, and Sparkly Martha knew this. Just the thought of touching a single grain of sand made Martha cringe. And now, it was everywhere! The place had been looking so lovely, too.

"Oh, cinnamon sticks!" Martha huffed. She looked at all the sand, shaking it from her hair, and shouted, "I'm just going to make you come back and clean it again!"

But—after Martha calmed down—she realized she may have been a little too harsh on her feisty helper. And the more she thought about it, a simple thank you wasn't a lot to ask, not for the overwhelming amount of cleaning that had just been done. She owed Sparkly Martha an apology, and she knew it. Martha had never meant to be so rude. She had only acted that way because she wanted everything to be perfect. These were very special guests she was expecting.

Her daughter, Jamie, was visiting Martha's new place for the first time with her two children, Lucas, who was nine, and Trinity, who was thirteen. Martha hadn't seen her grandchildren in the three months since the sudden death of their dad.

He'd recently been killed in the line of duty, where he worked as a police officer for the city. One night, at the end of his shift, he'd answered a call about a nearby building on fire. He was the closest officer and rushed over immediately. He was only supposed to secure the sight and wait for the fire department to show up. But as soon as he arrived, he heard people screaming. He couldn't ignore them. So he disregarded protocol and rushed into the burning building without a second thought. He blindly fought his way through smoke and flames, frantically following the screams. Heroically, he saved a young girl and her mother from certain death. Tragically, however, he was unable to save himself. He ran back into the building, thinking he'd heard another scream. The woman and child he'd just saved assured him no one else was in the building, but he had to be sure for himself. The building had collapsed seconds after, trapping him inside, and he'd perished in the fire. The firefighters who'd arrived shortly after quickly extinguished the fire. They searched and searched the burnt rubble but never found his body—only his badge.

After the funeral, Martha sold her house in the city and bought an old orphanage that had recently closed. It was located in the country, in a small, hilly town that wasn't on any map. She'd moved hundreds of miles away without explanation and now lived about twenty-five miles from the Square, surrounded by farmland and greenery as far as the eye could see. She'd kept the orphanage as it was, a modest two-story white farmhouse with a green shingled roof and a wraparound porch, all of which rested on a sprawling fifty acres. She even kept the original nasty-looking mustard-green wallpaper on the inside, plastered everywhere throughout the house. The only thing she'd added was outside. Since her land was open and bordered by everything green (green trees, green leaves, and green grass), she'd decided to throw in a splash of color. So she grew and maintained a neat and prim little garden nearby, filled with roses, dandelions, and a handful of scattered wildflowers. Next to that garden was a giant, magnificent-looking oak tree. This tree was a wondrous sight and stood taller than any other tree for miles. It may have been the most spectacular tree in all of Texas. And under that big, beautiful oak tree was a small bench, with just enough room for two, next to a quiet pond filled with plump fish.

But buying this old orphanage and moving so far away was

only the beginning of Martha's surprises. That was because she'd decided she would finally reveal to her grandchildren that she was a witch. She had already revealed this to her daughter years ago, but Jamie had never believed her. She knew her mom *identified* as a witch but never thought she *was* one. To this day, she truly believed her mom was outright out of her mind and off her rocker! *And maybe she was.* But Martha wasn't only going to share her secret with her grandchildren; she was going to give them a little taste of it, too—*literally*. She wanted to brighten their spirits using her magic and had something extra special planned.

Martha would have to apologize to Sparkly Martha at a later time; before she could summon her again, her guests suddenly pulled into the driveway. They'd arrived earlier than expected.

But Martha couldn't go outside to greet them yet either; she needed to quickly get rid of all the sand still scattered everywhere. So she reached into her hair and pulled out a seemingly ordinary farm-fresh chicken's egg to get the job done. But this egg was far from ordinary. It was magical, filled with a unique and unusual potion instead of a yolk.

She raised the egg as high as her arms could reach, ready to slam it to the ground, but instead, she cracked it open ever so gently with her fingers. As she split the shell in half, out fell a teensy-weensy speckled-colored chicken, no bigger than a marble—*and it was alive!* Martha made clucking sounds at the chicken, which clucked back as if it understood her. *Cluck cluck. Cluck cluck.* It then ruffled its tiny feathers and began pecking at the sand on the floor, one grain at a time. *Cluck.* Peck. *Cluck.* Peck. *Cluck.* Peck. But the chicken was moving too slowly. Martha needed all of the sand picked up *now.* So she gave the bird a little nudge. She lifted her foot, clucking loudly—and slammed it down on the chicken, pulverizing the poultry! *Baaacluuuck!* But the chicken escaped from under her boot unharmed. After all, this was a magical chicken. Instead of being squished, the chicken exploded into a blanket of dazzling fluorescent pink fog that raced to cover all the loose sand everywhere in the house, including the sand in her hair.

Once the fog touched each grain of sand, it then acted like metal to a magnet and—*shwoomp!*—stuck itself to the ceiling, hiding from plain sight. It wasn't perfect, but it was good enough for now. *Out of sight, out of mind*, Martha thought.

CHAPTER THREE
BUBBLES

Upon arrival, Jamie was the first to step foot on Martha's new property. She opened the door and hopped out of Big Blue—the nickname of the old station wagon she drove. Lucas and Trinity were still napping from the long trip—Lucas in the backseat and Trinity in the front. Jamie hadn't seen much of the countryside of Texas. She was a city girl through and through, which was why she was so shocked to discover that her mom had decided to buy an old orphanage *and* open a coffee shop, in the middle of nowhere, on a whim.

Pushing her strong skepticism aside, Jamie would be lying if she said she wasn't taken aback by the beauty of it all. The country was completely different from the cluster of the city. The grass and leaves were lush and green, and the sky was open and blue, not a cloud in sight. As she closed her eyes to take it all in, a calming fresh breeze brushed through her strawberry-blonde hair, and the warmth from the sun caressed her face. She didn't realize it, but for a moment, she was smiling, something she hadn't done in the three months since her husband died in that awful fire.

But as soon as Jamie opened her eyes and noticed her mom standing on the porch with a frustratingly familiar enthusiastic look, that moment was gone. Jamie stopped smiling and braced herself. She may have been a small-framed woman, but underneath, she had the ferociousness of a momma bear when need be, and though this might not have been one of those moments, a little bit of her momma bear came out—as it usually did *any time* she had an encounter with her *own* mom.

Here we go, Jamie thought, and with heavy feet, trudged forward. "Ma," she said with an uncertain tone as she approached her mom. She had been dreading this moment. She dug her hands deep into the back pockets of her pants. "Still wearing the patch, I see," she mumbled.

Martha paced her speed for dramatic effect as her feet carried her down the many porch steps—*all three*.

She reached her arms out to welcome Jamie. "Hey, pumpkin," Martha said with a country hello. "Did you have any trouble finding the place?"

"No trouble at all," Jamie answered.

Martha gave her a great big hug and squeezed her tightly.

"Okaaay," Jamie said as she wiggled from her mom's grip.

"Sorry," Martha said with a smile. "But after the morning I've had, *you* are a welcomed sight for sore eyes. Being a witch is exhausting, I tell you. It's not all it's made out to be, you know. I had to turn another boy into a frog today to get him to eat his vegetables. That makes thirteen this month alone. I swear by a troll's toe. I *really am* considering retirement."

And just like that, it felt like old times. Jamie rolled her eyes. *Here we go again with the witch stuff,* she thought—*bunch of nonsense.*

"I'm serious," Martha continued. "It's a full-time job."

Jamie rolled her eyes again. "You're not a witch, Ma," she said.

"Believe what you want," Martha told her. "Either way, I have decided that while you and the kids are here, I'm going to tell them the truth. The timing feels right."

Jamie squinted. She didn't like where this was going. "What truth?" she asked with concern, already well aware of what her mom would say next, though she hoped she was wrong.

"That I'm a witch, of course," Martha replied.

"Oh geez!" Jamie said. "Not this again. Please don't start with that garbage. I didn't want you to tell them the other twenty times you thought it was the *'right time,'* and I certainly don't want you to tell them now. Come on! You're not a witch, Ma!"

"I am, too," Martha insisted. "I've been trying to tell you for over forty years. You just refuse to believe it. But it's high time my grandchildren knew the truth, whether *you* believe it or not."

"First of all," Jamie said. "I'm *not* over forty. And if you're a witch—show me a magic trick."

Gasp! Martha placed her hand on her chest in shock. "That's blasphemy!" she shouted. "I am, too, a witch, and I do real magic, *not tricks!*"

"OK then," Jamie snarked. "Show me some *real* magic. And pulling things from your hair doesn't count. I could hide things too if I had *that* much hair."

"No," Martha huffed with her arms folded. "You're a condescending grump, and I don't want to."

"Of course, you don't," Jamie said sarcastically. *"How convenient."*

"It's true," Martha said. "You need to accept that I am who I am before I show you any of *my* magic."

"Whatever," Jamie said. "Identify however you want. But we both know you are *no witch*. And you're not a pirate. So you can lose that hideous eye patch."

"I made this eye patch myself, thank you very much—and I need it," Martha assured her.

"You don't need it!" Jamie argued.

"I *do so* need it!" Martha claimed as she slid the patch to the other eye. *"And I like it."*

Jamie huffed. "You look like a fortune teller from a B-rated horror movie," she stated rudely.

"Well," Martha said softly but confidently, "everyone knows the best fortune tellers live here in Texas."

Jamie squeezed her head like she was about to pop it off and snarled like a raging bull.

"You're not a fortune teller either, Ma!"

"I never said I was," Martha argued. *"But I am a witch."*

"No, you're not, Ma!"

"Yes, I am, Jamie."

"*No, Ma, you're not!*"

"Yes, Jamie, I am. No toil, no trouble, no boil, no bubbles. How would I know that if I wasn't a witch? That's something only witches say." Martha lifted her chin. "Just for the record," she added, "you can never repeat those words around any other witch. Seriously! I can say it, but you can't."

Crazy old bat, Jamie thought. She still had a few choice words she wanted to scream at her mom but held her tongue. "Listen," she said. "I only brought the kids out here this weekend for a distraction. *That's all.* They don't need anything extra on their plates right now. So I'm begging you, for once, can you at least pretend to be a normal, ordinary grandmother while we're here—for their sake— please?" She looked her mom up and down, knowing that was a tall order, and rephrased. "As ordinary as possible."

Martha looked at Jamie with endearment. She placed her hands on Jamie's shoulders, staring deeply into her eyes—the way only a mother knows how. "I know things are hard right now. And I know the sadness you and the kids carry is a heavy one. I carry it too. But they lost their father. Nothing is going to distract them from that."

Then, out of nowhere, Martha clapped with excitement, changing the tone completely—*clap, clap*—and whispered with enthusiasm, "I almost forgot."

Her shoulders jumped as her eyes popped, and she cracked an awkward grin. "There's someone I want to introduce you to."

Really? Jamie thought. *Right now? Who could that be?*

Martha bowed and twirled her hands in a fancy manner, gesturing a royal introduction as if she were introducing the queen herself. "Allow me to properly introduce you. Bubbles, meet Jamie. Jamie, meet Bubbles."

Jamie looked around—but saw no one.

"Is Bubbles invisible?" she asked sarcastically.

"Behind you, dear," Martha replied with a nod.

OK, I'll play along, Jamie thought as she turned with annoyance. But never in a million years did she expect to see what she saw. "Geez!" she yipped. She was so startled she jumped back, almost jumping out of her shoes. "What the heck is that thing?"

"That's Bubbles," Martha answered.

"Is that—*a goat?*" Jamie asked in disbelief.

"Well, she's not a cat." Martha chuckled. But Jamie didn't chuckle back.

This goat was, by far, undeniably, the *ugliest, most hideous, most absolutely revolting* goat Jamie had ever seen! She wasn't even sure it was a goat at all. Bubbles was completely bald. She didn't have a single hair on her body, not so much as a whisker on her chin, only dry saggy skin, all pink and wrinkly, like an experiment gone terribly wrong. And it was a wonder how she held herself up. Her knees knocked together when she walked, and her legs were so skinny and bowed they wobbled like rubber. Her hooves looked like giant chunks of coal, and she had two misshapen horns that twisted into themselves like a deformed clump of melted clay. Her jaw hung open constantly as flies buzzed around the food stuck between her big blocky teeth. And everywhere she went, she dragged her swollen, leaky udders on the ground, leaving behind a stinky trail of curdled milk that smelled worse than goblin diarrhea.

Bubbles was unnatural looking, to say the least, and if that wasn't bad enough, she also had the biggest, bulgiest, roundest eyes Jamie had ever seen before—but those were a result of the glasses the goat wore. That's right—glasses! Bubbles had to wear them because her eyes crossed and wandered, causing her to bump into things constantly.

Martha told Jamie her elaborate story of how she'd made the spectacles herself, using metal coat hangers from her closet to construct the frames and two old clunky magnifying glasses from her hair for the lenses. She'd then glued it all together using an entire bottle of Witch's Glue (not sold in stores). Once it dried, she'd strapped the entire contraption over Bubbles's horns. In the end, it seemed to help with her overall vision. Of course, she wouldn't be winning a beauty pageant anytime soon, but she wasn't bumping into things anymore, and that was all that mattered.

Jamie wasn't holding back her thoughts. "Disgusting," she cried. "Absolutely disgusting! Where on earth did you find such a beast? That is the ugliest goat I've ever seen in my life."

As Jamie went on and on with her harsh and ugly words, Bubbles sure seemed insulted—*incredibly insulted*. What a thing to say! She cocked her jaw to the side as far as it would go and stared at Jamie with daggers in her big bulging eyes, a creepy stare, never blinking or looking away once. "Mahahahaha," she bleated, which, *in goat,* meant, "I'm going to get you!"

CHAPTER FOUR
YELLOW RAIN

Lucas and Trinity were now waking up.

"Wow!" Lucas said, rubbing his face and yawning with a quick stretch. "This place is huge!"

He sprang forward, excited to get a better look—*completely forgetting the window was there*—and smashed his nose against the glass, knocking his glasses off his face.

"I'm OK," he said. He picked up his glasses and readjusted them. The right lens had a small crack that had been there for some time, but now, it was much more noticeable after smashing them against the window.

Trinity rolled her eyes. "You're such a nerd," she said with seemingly no emotion while turning to look out her own window—*without* smashing her face.

Lucas noticed his mom and grandmother talking by the porch. "Hey, there's Grandma!" he shouted with excitement. He sprang forward, this time forgetting he was still buckled in, and his glasses came off again.

"I'm OK," he said once more as he picked up his glasses and readjusted them a second time.

"Whatever," Trinity grumbled. "Let's just get this nightmare over with."

"Nightmare?" Lucas disagreed. "This isn't going to be a nightmare. It's Grandma! It's going to be fun! I can't wait to see what she'll pull from her hair *this* time."

"Whatever," she grumbled again as they both exited the car.

The second Martha saw her grandchildren from afar, her eyes *lit up* and sparkled like diamonds. She clenched her hands tightly with excitement and pressed them against her chest. She couldn't wait to wrap them both in her arms with great big, back-crunching Grandma hugs.

But before that could happen, Jamie took a deep breath and stood directly in front of her mom. "Please keep it simple this weekend," she pleaded once more. "None of this nonsense about witches and magic and tricks with your hair. And keep that chupacabra *you* call a goat away from my children. It could have rabies."

What a request, Martha thought. It was like getting slapped with a big smelly fish and being told not to stink.

But she didn't argue. "I promise," she agreed as she pretended to zip her lips, lock them, and throw away the key. But Martha was sneaky. She had her fingers crossed the entire time, *triple-crossed* the way witches do. They both turned, wearing fake smiles, and faced the kids.

Martha stretched her neck over to Jamie, muttering quickly out of the side of her mouth one last time, "I am a witch, though."

That sent Jamie over the edge. "Grrrrr!" she grunted in anger as she lost her patience and exploded, throwing her hands in the air. "**You're not a witch, Ma!**"

Lucas heard the yelling. "Did Mom just call Grandma the B word?" he asked Trinity, chuckling as he grabbed his and his mom's suitcase from the back of Big Blue.

"Who cares?" Trinity replied as she circled in place, holding her phone in the air for a better signal. "Get my suitcase too," she commanded.

"Get your own suitcase," he mumbled under his breath—*way, way* under.

"Excuse me?" she said fiercely, about to erupt like a volcano.

"Nothing," he quickly replied as he reluctantly grabbed her suitcase.

As Lucas struggled to close the hatch, he noticed Trinity staring at an old rusty scratch under the right tail light, a scratch she'd caused with her bike years ago. He remembered how she'd cried that day, not because she was hurt but because she thought she would be in big trouble.

When their dad had found the scratch, he smiled and told Trinity, "Don't worry, bug. Big Blue can handle it."

He'd pinky swore he wouldn't tell Mom and that he would take the blame if she ever found the scratch. "But next time, I'll have to arrest you," he joked.

It was a good memory. But then again, all memories of their dad were good.

"You, OK?" Lucas asked.

"Just leave me alone," she said as she stomped away.

Lucas took a deep breath and placed his hand on Big Blue. "She just misses you, Dad." He sighed. "We all do."

Deep down, Trinity was happy to see her grandmother but remained guarded and didn't show it. Since her dad's death, she had become reclusive. She was tall and slim but hid under dark frumpy sweaters and a slouched posture. She'd even quit the cheerleading team she was captain of and dyed her natural blond hair black. She kept it pulled back in a single tight ponytail. And like her mom, but with reasons of her own, Trinity wasn't very receptive to her grandmother's happy greeting. So she gave her a formal handshake instead.

"You look different," Martha pointed out.

"You don't," Trinity said. "Still wearing the patch, huh?"

Martha slid her eye patch to the other eye. "Yes, I am," she answered proudly, her chin high. "Glad to have you at my humble abode. *Nothing unusual happening here.*" She turned and gave an obvious and sarcastic wink to Jamie. "Just your regular, old, average, normal grandmother. Nothing more. Doot da doot da doot. Just being ordinary. Doot da doot da dooty doo."

"Ummm, OK? That's cool," Trinity said, puzzled but not enough to care. "Cool dog, too," she added casually. She was, of course, referring to Bubbles the goat. She pulled out her phone and snapped a quick photo before walking away. She was constantly taking random photos like that.

"Jeez, Ma!" Jamie shrieked, startled after another look at Bubbles. "That thing gives me the heebie-jeebies. You should put that beast out of its misery."

Martha ignored Jamie.

"I guess just make yourself at home!" she shouted as Trinity walked inside the house and shut the door.

Well, that didn't go how I expected it would, Martha thought as she turned her attention to Lucas. *He* had not changed one bit since she'd seen him last. He still had the same messy blond hair as his dad's, wore the same goofy red glasses *too big for his face,* and was still very small and scrawny for a nine-year-old. Martha thought he looked as though he may have gotten smaller. And he was still meticulous with how he dressed—T-shirt tucked into jean shorts, suspenders on top, white socks pulled to his knees, and penny loafer shoes on his feet, with a shiny new penny in each shoe. The suspenders and penny loafers belonged to his dad. They didn't fit him too well, but he wore them anyway, proudly too. Lucas had kept many of his dad's things after he died. His favorite thing, though, which he carried everywhere, was his dad's police badge. He never left the house without it.

Martha noticed how, unlike Trinity, Lucas openly showed his excitement. His shoulders were raised back as he stood strong, proudly carrying three suitcases like it was a piece of cake. And his wonderfully cheerful smile made his freckled cheeks glow like two perfect pink moons.

As he approached his mom and grandmother, though, that "piece of cake" began weighing down on him.

Lucas's legs buckled, and his arms grew weak. *Uh-oh*, he thought. He'd known the suitcases were too heavy when he'd grabbed them from the car. Each bag weighed more than he did, but he'd tried to carry them anyway. Big beads of sweat rolled down his face as he clenched his teeth, trying to hide his trembling. He was almost there—until he stumbled in his dad's shoes and tripped over a big rock hiding in the grass.

Down he went!

Lucas hit the ground face-first, and his legs went flying over his head. The suitcases came crashing down next, right on top of him, one after the other. This startled Bubbles, who let out a loud "Mahahahaha!" before she bounced away, frantically hopping out of sight.

"I'm OK," Lucas confirmed as he sat up. He pushed his glasses to his face and wiped the grass and dirt from his knees and elbows. Luckily, none of it got on his white socks.

"Of course you are," Martha said as she walked over and assisted him to his feet.

"Did I hear a goat?" Lucas asked, looking up at his grandmother.

"Yes, you did," she replied. "Good ear. But Bubbles is no ordinary goat."

"You got that right," Jamie scoffed as she walked away to answer her phone. She rolled her eyes at her mom once more before taking the call.

"Ignore your mother," Martha said to Lucas with a smile. She leaned over and whispered in his ear, "Bubbles is a *magical* goat."

Lucas smiled with wonder. His big blue eyes sparkled behind those even bigger round frames.

That's when Martha noticed the crack in his lens. "Want me to fix that?"

"Fix what?" he asked.

"Your broken headlight, silly," she answered, pointing at his glasses.

"How are you going to do that?" he asked, crossing his eyes to look down.

"I'll show you how." Martha grabbed Lucas's glasses from his face. She licked her thumb like she was licking a stamp and then rubbed the crack, smearing her spit across the lens.

"Take this glass that's round and cracked. Let my spit—fix it back."

Suddenly, the wind shifted, strengthening each time her thumb passed over the crack. The quiet sky quickly filled with birds chirping loudly, in a synchronized melody Lucas had never before heard, as they scattered from the trees. It was as if the birds were truly singing a song.

Tweedly deedly tweet tweet tweet. Tweedly deedly tweet. Tweedly deedly tweet tweet tweet. Tweedly deedly tweet.

Lucas looked up and all around. He couldn't see a thing without his glasses, only blurry smudges of images, but he knew something was happening—*and it felt magical.*

Martha took a huge deep breath like she was about to blow with the unstoppable force of a thousand hurricanes, but she puckered her lips instead and gently puffed a single soft breath—*puff*—directly on the crack, just enough to fog the lens for a brief moment. The wind immediately stopped, and the birds went silent. Then . . .

Bam!

The wind came roaring back, and the birds were now louder than ever, singing *tweedly deedly tweet* repeatedly! Leaves and grass swirled and twirled around Lucas, lifting him ever so slightly in the air. His toes were inches from the grass, but only briefly before he was gently dropped back down to the ground. Then, just like that, the magic was over—and it was a wonder Jamie didn't notice any of it happening.

"There you go," Martha said. She returned Lucas his glasses, but not before polishing the lenses with a little magic from one of her wild curls—that way, they would never scratch or crack again. *She used her hair for everything.*

Lucas was speechless. He put his glasses on joyfully as he pulled leaves and grass from his hair.

"It's gone!" he shouted. He took them off again and looked at the lens closely to be sure. Then he put them back on. "How'd you do that?"

"Magic," she whispered with her finger over her lips. She lifted her eye patch with a flick, winked, and then slid it over to the other eye as she lowered it back down.

Lucas giggled, pushing his glasses to his face. "Thanks, Grandma!" he said with excitement as he tried to wink back, blinking both eyes instead, and gave her a big hug.

"You're very welcome," she said with a smile. "Now, let's get you inside."

As they walked together, Lucas noticed his dad's shoes, now, all of a sudden—*fit perfectly*. He looked up at his grandmother with his mouth open, about to ask if she had done that too, but she was one step ahead and spoke before he could ask.

"Well," she said, lifting her patch again, this time with a double wink before lowering it back down. "We can't have you tripping everywhere you go."

Lucas smiled, and the two continued inside.

Just moments after her mom and Lucas had gone in the house, a frustrated Jamie finished her phone call and soon followed behind them. She stopped on the porch, closed her eyes, and took a deep breath before walking inside. *This weekend is going to be a long one,* she thought. After exhaling, with her eyes still closed, a warm, wet feeling washed over her head and ran down her entire body—and it *wasn't* a good feeling. It happened so horribly fast, she had no time to move a single muscle before it was over. *What is this?* she thought.

Sniff. Sniff. Whatever it was, it smelled foul and wretched, like it had crawled up her nose and died. It was awful! *Just awful!* Even worse, she was foolish enough to lick her lips to taste whatever it was she'd been doused in. The dry, burning, bitter flavor zapped her taste buds and paralyzed her tongue. Once she could wipe her eyes and withstand the burn, she opened them and looked up.

"Ahhhhhhhhhhhhh!" she screamed.

Jamie was beyond mad at this point. Her face went red, and her veins throbbed like a hundred pounding war drums. "You gotta be kidding me!" she shouted. She clutched her hands tightly and shook them wildly in the air as if she was choking two invisible chickens. She looked like she was about to have a nervous breakdown—*if she wasn't already having one.*

You see, Bubbles was on the roof of the house, taking aim at Jamie below—*and laughing too.* "Ma ha ha, ma ha ha!"

Jamie was soaked, dripping from head to toe, and unfortunately, it wasn't Bubbles's stinky curdled milk that had saturated her; it was Bubbles's other liquid—*the yellow kind*—the kind no one ever ever ever wants to be covered in—*ever!* And now Jamie was—a showering amount of it too. Bubbles "got her," after all.

CHAPTER FIVE

MAGIC CAKE? BIG MISTAKE!

Jamie entered the house in a quiet rage. Her shoes sloshed as she angrily wiped them on the black rubber mat in the doorway. Funny enough, the mat read: "Don't wipe TOO hard."

Martha was in the far corner of the living room, sitting in her favorite blue recliner, squeaking against the old torn leather with each movement she made. She was hunched under a hook-shaped lamp with hanging tassels, sewing a bunch of black eye patches and stuffing them into her hair one by one as she finished.

Lucas was resting on his elbows, sprawled out by her feet on the dark hardwood floor, and looking through an old photo album.

He was the first to look up. "Why are you all wet?" Lucas asked his mom. "Is it raining?"

"No, it isn't raining," Jamie replied sternly, looking directly at *her* mom.

Martha laughed. "I see Bubbles got you," she said.

"*Got me?*" Jamie asked, angry as she dripped yellow drops in the doorway. "She didn't *get* me! She peed on my head from the rooftop! A bucket's worth of bodily fluids all over me, Ma! Like all over!" She gestured with her hands, pointing to the parts of her body that would need extra washing in the shower. "How on earth did your stupid goat get on the roof, to begin with?"

"I have no idea." Martha chuckled. She looked at Lucas, lifting her eye patch with a wink before lowering it back down and whispering, "Goat magic."

"I'm glad you find it funny, Ma!" Jamie thundered.

"I'm sorry," Martha said, trying to control her chuckling.

"Whatever," Jamie huffed. "Where's your bathroom?"

"At the end of the hall, dear." Martha pointed with her needle in hand.

But before going to the bathroom, Jamie angrily slipped each of her shoes off by the heel using only the force of her feet so she wouldn't have to touch them with her hands. She then looked down at her nasty socks and wiggled her gross wet toes in disgust. She tried to slip them off the same way she had with her shoes, but the socks were too slippery. She only rubbed the foul smell deeper into her skin. She didn't want to but knew she had to use her hands. So, with hesitation, she gripped a fist and grunted and, using only the tips of her fingers, quickly ripped them off. A wide, yellow cloud of mist could be seen as each sock left her foot.

"I'm sure Bubbles meant no harm," Martha assured Jamie. "I'm sure she was only playing. You know. Like, tag, you're it."

"Seriously?" Jamie asked. She squinted her eyes and slightly tilted her head. "Are you honestly comparing what your stupid goat did to me—*to a game of tag*?"

Martha pondered her logic for a second. "Well," she said. "When you put it like that."

"So what then?" Jamie interrupted. "Am I supposed to pee on *her* now?"

Gasp! Martha's jaw dropped. "As if!" she replied. "Have some class! You can't just go around peeing on things whenever you feel like it. What are you, an animal?" She chuckled again, this time under her breath, trying to keep a serious face, but she just couldn't hold back her laughter.

Lucas joined in, laughing as well.

Jamie didn't find any of this funny, not one bit. "I'm glad you both think it's so amusing," she said as she stuffed her wet, smelly, disgusting socks into her shoes. They made a sloshy, squishy-squashing squidgy sound as they went in. "Let *me* pee on one of *you* and see if you're still laughing then."

Martha and Lucas stopped laughing at exactly the same time. They looked at each other with seriousness—then at Jamie—and then both exploded into uncontrollable laughter once more. Tears and snot ran down their faces. They were laughing so hard they couldn't catch their breath.

Jamie dropped her shoes on the mat in a tantrum, grabbed her bag, and stormed off in anger straight to the bathroom. Her thoughts quickly drifted toward her husband. For a split second, she thought this moment, though embarrassing and disgusting for her, would've been hilarious to him. He was always able to find the humor in just about everything. And maybe if he was still alive, even *she* could've seen the humor in being peed on by a bald goat wearing glasses. But he wasn't, and she didn't.

Halfway down the dimly lit hall, a single framed photo on the wall caught Jamie's eye and distracted her thoughts. She crumpled the knitted runner beneath her feet as she stopped suddenly and stared. In the photo was a young boy wearing a pair of thrashed overalls covered in mud. He stood knee-deep in a small pond, holding onto a fat little fish with both hands. The boy seemed familiar, though she'd never seen this photo before. She didn't know why, but the longer she stared at it, the sadder she became—until she noticed her reflection in the glass. The second she saw her soiled, wet, yellow-dripping hair, she quickly stormed off in anger again. She slammed the door once she was inside the bathroom.

Trinity heard the slam but ignored it. She was alone, sitting in an old wooden rocker beside the bed, rocking back and forth and staring out the window at the trees. She had chosen one of the many rooms in the house to hide away in. For such a small house, there was quite a bit of space. She stayed sitting, holding her phone in her lap, with an image of her dad on the home screen. Every thirty seconds, the screen would dim, and she would tap it and cry. "I miss you so much," she whispered, sobbing softly and wiping her tears on her sweater. She rocked back and forth, back and forth, back and forth, and continued to stare out the window.

Meanwhile, without so much as a clue, Martha was brewing up trouble—*terrible trouble*. And it'd begun brewing long before this moment. She noticed Lucas was almost finished flipping through the photo album. He was on the last few pages when she leaned forward. "Psssssst, Lucas," she whispered.

"Yeah, Grandma?" he replied, looking up at her.

She sat up and looked around, making sure the coast was clear. Then, she quickly shoved the rest of the patches she was holding, along with her needle and thread, deep into her hair. It's a wonder how she didn't poke herself.

Once Martha knew for certain they were alone, she leaned forward again, closer this time. "I have something important I want to tell you and your sister," she whispered. "It's a secret, so we'll have to keep it hush-hush. I don't want your mom to find out."

"I love secrets, Grandma," he said. He closed the photo album and pushed it aside.

"Of course you do," Martha replied. "And I have a whopper of a secret to tell. But first, I have a very special gift I've personally prepared for both you and your sister to share."

"What is it?"

"I'll show you."

Martha paused to build the anticipation, then reached into her hair, elbow deep in that thick, curly mess, her tongue slanted out of her mouth, and she pulled out a small transparent glass plate. But the plate wasn't the gift. The gift was *on* the plate.

It was a stupendous, astonishing, unbelievably extraordinary, marvelous slice of cake!

But this wasn't your average grocery store cake. No. Far from it. This beauty was a three-layer slice of the fluffiest white cake in all existence, topped and filled with the brightest blue icing one could imagine, bluer than the bluest oceans, and whipped to perfection. It had just the right cake-to-icing ratio and was cut in the most perfect triangular shape. It was a thing of magnificence.

From the moment Martha found out her grandchildren were coming to visit, she'd worked tirelessly, day and night, to conjure and create this *one slice of cake*. It was remarkable. And the plate this piece of cake sat on was no ordinary plate either. It had been engraved with magical writing along the border.

She had given it her all for days, using every bit of magic she possessed, including multiple spells, potions, and chants. The ingredients alone had taken weeks to gather. Sure, there were some basic ingredients, such as flour, sugar, milk, butter, and eggs, that were easy to come by. But the *key ingredients*, now those were nearly impossible to find. They included:

— *four whiskers from a dead cat that's been buried twice;*

— *chicken bones ground to a powder in a stone bowl while dancing;*

— *ginger root grown in a graveyard and plucked under a full moon at exactly midnight;*

— *and, last but not least, a week's worth of fingernails from a newborn baby.*

Martha had almost been arrested trying to acquire that last ingredient. She'd even made it in the local paper. The headline read:

"The Fingernail Bandit Strikes Again."

But it was all worth it in the end. Besides, she was never actually identified as the bandit. And now she was able to see the joy in her grandchildren's eyes as she presented her gift.

The sweet aroma filled Lucas's nose and grabbed hold of his taste buds. It was as though he could taste the cake by smelling it! It was an absolute masterpiece. But the surprise got even better.

"That—looks—*so good!*" Lucas said, drooling uncontrollably. He wanted to gobble it down more than anything.

"Oh, it's *yummy*, for sure!" Martha told him. "And it's magical."

Lucas leaned forward. He pushed his glasses to his face and licked his lips.

"This cake holds great power," Martha foretold. "It grants wishes! With just one bite of this cake, you could have almost anything you wanted in the entire world. Whatever your heart desires. All you need to do is make a wish."

Lucas *sprang up*, sitting with his legs crisscrossed, gripped with excitement. His eyes grew wide. He couldn't wait any longer. He simply had to have it! He reached his hands out, but Martha pulled back.

"Nah-ah-ah," she said. "Not yet."

Martha placed the plate on her lap for a quick second and gave her gloves a dainty tug. Then, after picking up the plate, she mystically waved her hand over the cake, snapped her fingers with rhythm, and hummed like she was about to begin singing an oldies doo-wop—*snap! hmm, hm, snap! hmm, hm, snap! hmm, hm*—and the engravings on the plate *lit up.*

Lucas gazed upon the blinding, glimmering glow with great fascination. It almost seemed like he was in a trance, hypnotized, dreaming about stuffing this cake down his gullet and how it would taste.

Martha warned there could be dire consequences if she didn't read the engravings carefully before the cake was eaten. Lucas nodded as if he understood but didn't seem to be paying attention. He was a prisoner to his stomach, and this cake was his salvation. But Martha needed both grandchildren to hear the words together at the same time since it was a gift meant for the two of them. So she placed the cake on the small table next to her chair, hopped up, and quickly shuffled to fetch Trinity. Her rags dragged behind her as she hurried off.

Big mistake!

When Martha returned with Trinity mere seconds later, she found Lucas sitting there with a guilty smile, stretched from ear to ear—and he was licking his lips with satisfaction and delight. *Ahhhh.*

"Oh, cinnamon sticks," Martha mumbled to herself. "That's not good."

"Ugh," Trinity said as she snapped a quick photo of Lucas, who was a mess.

"Sorry, Grandma," he said, slowly looking up at her. "I couldn't help myself."

Lucas's face and fingers were completely covered in blue icing. There seemed to be more icing on *him* than there ever was on the cake, to begin with. Martha looked down at the plate, which looked like it had been licked clean by a pack of hungry hounds. The entire piece of cake was gone, and Lucas was swallowing the last bite. To top it all off, the engravings on the plate were no longer glowing or glimmering, which could only mean one thing—a wish had been made.

CHAPTER SIX
ONE BIG WISH

Martha knew better than to leave a slice of cake in front of Lucas and not expect him to eat it, especially a magical slice that grants wishes. She should've been more careful. *Silly witch!* Her intentions were good, but her planning was poor. She'd meant for Lucas to share the cake with his sister, and neither was supposed to eat the entire piece! A single bite was all it would take for the magic to work; any more beyond that was far too dangerous. But Martha's plan had failed—*miserably*.

The engravings on the plate had been placed there by Martha to guarantee Lucas and Trinity's safety—filtering out and then blocking any and all outrageous or boneheaded wishes (a fool's wish), the kind any kid might make. It was meant to keep them out of harm's way from dangerous wishes as well. It was Martha's version of a magical child safety lock—to protect them from themselves. But without her reading those words, there was no limit to what one could wish for. The endless possibilities raced through Martha's head. She knew that whatever might happen next was ultimately out of her hands. And before she could say or do anything, something *did* happen.

Chugga chugga, choo ooooooooo! An unbearably loud sound, like the piercing whistle and chugga chugga chugging of a speeding locomotive, filled everyone's ears, pounding at their eardrums, and the entire house began to rumble and shake!

The floors creaked like crazy, and the walls ran with splitting cracks that popped through the ugly brittle wallpaper. Books rattled off the shelves, and furniture slid all over the place, scuffing and scratching the floor, shredding the hardwood surface into curling peels like a pencil sharpener. Dishes fell out of the cabinet by the dozen, porcelain cups, ceramic plates, and glass bowls, most shattering to bits as they hit the floor. The ceiling itself seemed like it was about to cave in.

Martha quickly grabbed her grandchildren and brought them to the center of the living room. "Down!" she shouted. "Get down!"

Lucas and Trinity quickly dropped to the floor, covering their heads as they huddled beside her. Martha remained standing, trying to keep her balance in the middle of all the shaky movement and chaos. She hovered over them with her arms stretched wide.

"What's happening, Grandma?" Lucas shouted.

"Is it an earthquake?" Trinity shouted.

Their shouts sounded like whispers amid the noise. But Martha heard their voices. "This is no earthquake!" she assured them. "Hold on to my legs!"

Lucas and Trinity each grabbed a leg and held on tight.

Chugga chugga choo ooooooooo! Chugga chugga choo ooooooooo!

The house, all of a sudden, magically floated into the air. The loud whistling sound continued, growing louder and louder until the entire house and porch broke free from the ground with a loud *pop!* All the plumbing connected to the house snapped! As soon as that happened, the house went *flying* through the air, like it had been shot out of a giant catapult. It wobbled like a seesaw on a playground through the sky.

It flipped and twirled, the whole while spinning 'round and 'round. Faster and faster it spun, never slowing down once!

Lucas and Trinity screamed in a panic. Martha assured them everything was going to be OK. Holding on to her grandchildren for dear life, she quickly conjured up enough magic for one quick chant to make her hair grow. *And grow it did!*

"Listen, my curls, each and all. Grow for me now into a big ball!"

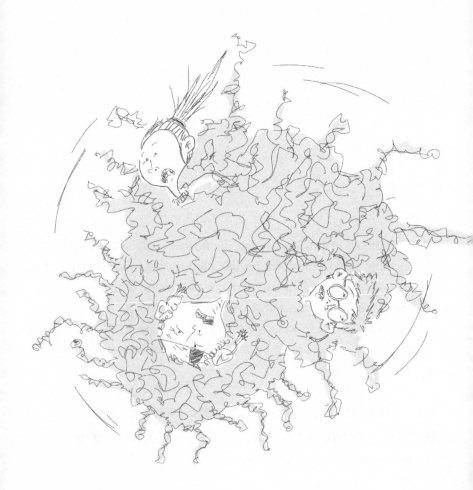

With that chant, each curly lock stretched long enough to wrap around Martha and her grandchildren multiple times, over and over, until they were wrapped tightly inside a giant hairball. But it didn't stop there. Her hair continued growing, growing, and growing, stretching far out to every corner until the entire room became a jungle of hair. With this final act of magic, Martha provided absolute safety using the cushion of her curls.

Jamie wasn't having such luck. She was still in the shower. She, too, was being tossed back and forth, shower wall to shower wall, *without* the cushion of a giant hairball. She was being smacked with shower toiletries left and right—soap in her eye, shampoo in her mouth, conditioner everywhere else, all while dodging a loose razor with Martha's hair on it. Worst of all, there was no water to rinse with! Thankfully, in a flash of blinding rainbow lights, everything suddenly stopped. It was as though time had paused momentarily, with everything in the house completely frozen. Then …

Ba-ba-ba boom!
The entire house slammed back down to the ground!

Once things seemed settled and Jamie had her footing, she bolted from the shower, slipping and sliding through the soapy mess. She quickly wrapped herself in a towel and ran to check on her kids. Everyone was OK, though, and for once, surprisingly enough, Lucas's glasses didn't budge from his face.

However, what Jamie saw next blew her mind! Martha's hair was moving, all on its own, like it was *alive*, each curl slithering like a snake back down to size.

Jamie pointed her finger at her mom. Her hand was shaking. *"You really are a w-w-witch?"* she yelled.

So many questions raced through her head. She tried to convince herself that what she had just seen wasn't possible and hadn't happened. "This isn't happening. This isn't happening. This isn't happening." But it *was* possible, and it *had* happened!

Martha shrugged with slight guilt. "Don't be mad," she told Jamie. "I did try to tell you—many times."

"And all this?" Jamie asked, still in shock, pointing to all the surrounding destruction. "Was this you? *Did you do this?*"

"Um, Mom? It was me," Lucas shamefully admitted.

"You?" Jamie asked, very surprised.

"Yeah, Mom," he confirmed. "I did this. I think I made a wish."

"A wish?" she asked. She was scared and so confused but frustrated too. "What do you mean you *think* you made a wish? And why is your face all blue?" She huffed and puffed. "First the goat and now this! Would somebody please tell me what's going on?"

"Wait," Trinity interrupted. "Goat? What happened with the goat?"

"That's not important right now," Jamie said.

"My goat peed on your mom, dear," Martha said nonchalantly.

"Gross, Mom!" Trinity said with disgust.

"Enough about the goat!" Jamie shouted.

"OK," Martha said defensively. "First of all. Her name is Bubbles. And yes, I may be a tad bit at fault here."

"A tad bit?" Jamie commented sarcastically.

"No, Mom," Lucas insisted. "Don't get mad at Grandma. She gave me some magic cake, *that's it*! The rest is my fault."

Jamie pressed her lips together and gave her mom the stink eye. *"Magic cake?* So you're just an accessory, then?" she asked, lowering her eyelids. "I knew coming here this weekend was a bad idea!"

Martha tried to explain. "I did give him the cake. But he wasn't supposed to eat it yet. I had a plan."

"You and your plans!" Jamie shouted. "It's always something with you!"

To make matters worse, the magic holding Sparkly Martha's sand to the ceiling had worn off—and it all fell at once. Considering everything else that had just taken place, a little sand didn't seem like that big a deal, not even to Martha, who absolutely hated the stuff—except Jamie was still dripping wet and covered in suds—and now sand! Unfortunately, that was the least of her problems. That was the least of any of their problems.

Lucas walked over to the window while his mom and grandmother continued arguing and peeked outside behind the curtains. "Yeesh," he said with uncertainty, his breath fogging up the glass. "Um, guys, you might wanna take a look at this. I don't think we're in Texas anymore."

You see, the moment Lucas devoured his grandmother's slice of magical cake, he'd only had one thought in mind: a memory of the time he and his dad had spent together at a medieval-themed carnival filled with knights and dragons and kings and castles. It was one of his favorite memories. And he wanted more memories like it. *He wanted his dad back.* He'd unknowingly wished he could go back in time, one day before his dad ran into that burning building and stop him from doing so. He desired this more than anything else in the entire world—and his wish had been granted.

However, he'd never made the wish out loud. He'd never even spoken a single word. Lucas's memory and his emotions were way more powerful than his words could *ever* be—so powerful, in fact, that his thoughts *became* the wish! And magic can be very unpredictable. Since he ate more cake than he was supposed to, that wish was amplified. His *one* wish was now like that of a *thousand*. Instead of going back just one day before his dad died, he went back years before that day, *many, many years*—to a place more like his memory.

Lucas had traveled through history on a riveting ride of magic—clear across the Atlantic and far from the comforts of Texas—back to a different time in history, a time when kings ruled the lands, a time when iron clanked against iron on the battlefield, and torches lit the night, a time long ago—*the Dark Ages*. Lucas had unexpectedly turned his grandmother's house into a giant time machine, magically zipping through centuries in seconds and landing all the way back in medieval times. But this was no carnival. This was real. And he'd brought his family with him!

"Oh, cinnamon sticks," Martha said. "Cinnamon cinnamon cinnamon sticks."

CHAPTER SEVEN
THE DUKE

Surprisingly, as remarkably unbelievable as it was, Martha's house had landed safely in one piece. Though an absolute mess inside, the outside was completely intact, not a single broken board or cracked window. Not one shingle was out of place. There wasn't even a scratch! But it wasn't *how* the house landed that was of any importance. It was *where* it landed—in the center of a small, isolated village. Tucked away in this village were a handful of tiny huts scattered about, huts that looked a lot like Martha's shop, the Witch's Brew. But these huts were mostly made of sticks and mud instead of stone. They had grass roofs instead of straw, and unlike Martha's coffee shop, these huts had no doors, just little openings that looked like they had been carved out by hand.

A grim and spooky forest surrounded most of the village, filled with giant, twisted, and mangled bulbous trees. Their leafless branches reached toward the sky like creepy clawed hands, completely blocking the sun. Only darkness survived beneath these trees—*darkness, and fear.*

71

The only way in or out of this village was a muddy path rarely traveled. It led far out to a small narrow bridge connecting to a hill. Just beyond that hill, a giant castle could be seen, where there was a great kingdom.

Martha took the lead, gathering everyone close and cautiously opening the door. She nervously stepped outside onto the porch. She didn't know what to expect. None of them did. Jamie and the kids slowly followed. As they all stepped out of the house, they entered a new and unknown world—one they were unprepared and ill-equipped for.

The air was wet and saturated in fog, making everything gloomy and gray. It was quiet and still—dead silence all around.

Lucas pushed his glasses to his face and wiped his lens. He was the first to notice movement through the fog.

He pointed. "What's that, Grandma?" he whispered. His whisper sounded like a shout.

Martha squinted. She saw it too.

Up ahead, there were two women, barefoot and tied to a tall wooden post. Each was clothed in what looked like an old, ragged potato sack, and they were as dirty as the day was long. They seemed to be the only two people around. The other villagers were nowhere to be seen, but their eyes could be felt, watching as they cowered in their huts.

Then, suddenly, from out of nowhere, a single soldier appeared on horseback, trotting toward the house, lifting the silence. He broke through the fog and approached. With her abilities, Martha was able to hear the haunting voices of the people this soldier had killed, looming over him from beyond the grave. His presence felt like a nightmare.

He was covered in black armor, plated with great big spikes, and stained with blood. His helmet cast a shadow over his eyes, concealing his face. He was enormous, twice the size of a regular man, and he carried a giant sword on his back, forged with all the broken blades of the fallen warriors he had conquered. This blade was strong and sharp enough to cut down an entire tree with a single swing. He was an evil man, battle-scarred and fierce-looking. He struck absolute terror and fear in all those who crossed his path.

He was known as—the Duke.

"Halt!" the Duke shouted. His voice was deep and raspy, and it carried far and wide. He pointed at the house, addressing Martha and her family. "What manner of madness is this?"

His armor wore heavy and restricted his movement; otherwise, he would've been able to look up and see the house fall from the sky.

Martha tried to come up with an explanation of how she and her family had ended up wherever—or whenever—they were. But there was no way for her to give any answer that would have sounded believable. Even if she told the truth and the Duke somehow believed her, it would've only made matters worse. Just looking around, Martha could tell things clearly worked differently here, especially for women. If a woman even thought about crossing the Duke, she imagined he would have no mercy in delivering a cruel, senseless, unjustified punishment, no questions asked, which is what she assumed had already happened to the two poor souls tied up. After all, this was the era of error.

Now, the king of these lands was fair and just. But he was a young king, no older than Lucas. His parents had died shortly after he was born, leaving him under the care of his uncle, the Duke, who'd raised him as his own. The king had no idea that people in his kingdom suffered under the Duke's reign of violence. The king only knew what the Duke told him. He was lied to and manipulated and innocently trusted the Duke with his life. The Duke also had the trust of the king's soldiers. Most respected him as a great warrior. Those who didn't—feared him for what they knew he was capable of doing—and *willing* to do. The Duke alone wielded the true power of the kingdom with his sword, and no man dared challenge him, king or commoner.

Martha's witch senses were tingling like crazy—and *they* sensed danger. She knew exactly what she needed to do at that moment. She only had one option—hightail her family out of there before something terrible happened! But how? And then she had a light bulb moment. *Aha!* she thought. She quickly darted off and ran inside her house in search of her broom. With her broom, she could travel hundreds of miles in the blink of an eye. She didn't know if it would help them get home to their *own time*, but she was certain it would get them to safety for now.

"Where does she think *she's* going?" Jamie asked with a high-pitched squeak. She hid behind her kids so she wouldn't be seen in only a bath towel.

Trinity and Lucas both shrugged. "I dunno," they said.

Martha searched her house, tossing things carelessly as she rummaged through the mess, but she couldn't find her broom. She tried to use her magic to locate it but was unable to do so. Then she remembered she'd left her broom on the porch. *Cinnamon sticks!* She thought. This was not good—no telling where it was now.

"Maaaaa—we could really use your help right now!" Jamie shouted.

"Stop your shouting, woman!" the Duke commanded, trotting forward, now right before them, only feet away. "Who are you, people? And where do you come from?"

"Where do *you* come from?" Trinity barked back, foolishly pulling out her phone and snapping a quick photo of him.

"Ummm, sweetheart?" Jamie whispered to Trinity, peeking over her shoulder. "I wouldn't do that if I were you."

"Do what?" Trinity asked, completely clueless.

Jamie pointed to the phone—*but it was too late.*

The Duke had already seen the *black magic box* in her hand. He reared back on his horse. *Clink, clink.* His armor clanked loudly. *Shing!*

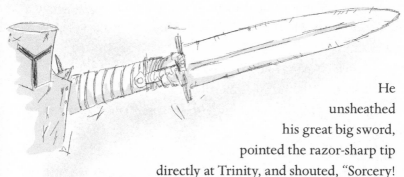

He
unsheathed
his great big sword,
pointed the razor-sharp tip
directly at Trinity, and shouted, "Sorcery!
She's a witch! Seize her! We'll tie her to the post with
the other two. We'll burn them all!"

Just then, twenty of the Duke's men appeared from behind
the heavy fog. They were common thugs and thieves, rotten, no-
good men without honor, cutthroats who blindly pledged their
allegiance for a mere price. They didn't wear armor and were not
trained or skilled in battle, but they carried weapons—swords and
axes—and they followed orders without question or hesitation.

Realizing her mistake, Trinity quickly shoved her phone
back into her pocket. "What do we do?" she called out to her
grandmother.

Martha heard the commotion and ran out of the house onto the
porch. She quickly ripped off her eye patch after noticing more men
on horses and threw it down. She could tell these vile vermin were
bad news. She needed both her eyes right now. She wouldn't admit
it to Jamie, but the eye patch was obstructing her vision.

"Grandma!" Lucas said. "Your eye patch!"

"I have plenty more," she assured him, pointing to her hair.

Lucas picked up the eye patch anyway and tucked it into his
shirt behind his suspender strap.

"I knew you didn't need that stupid patch," Jamie huffed,
tightening her towel.

"Now's not the time," Martha sang through her teeth.

"Just use some of that magic you're always bragging about!" Jamie shouted. "Do some witch stuff! You got us into this! Now get us out!"

"I can't," Martha said, worried how Jamie would respond.

"Why not?" Jamie asked sternly.

"Because," Martha answered after a pause, "I used all my magic on the cake."

"You did *what*?" Jamie shouted.

"I had to!" Martha declared. "I had to make sure each bite had an equal amount of my magic for the wishes to work properly."

"Yeah, a lot of good that did!" Jamie sarcastically pointed out.

"I know you're upset," Martha said. "But the bottom line is, I'm still recharging. Plus, I already told you I had to turn a boy into a frog earlier. That took magic too. And I fixed Lucas's glasses and made my hair grow. So I'm sorry, dear, but it will take some time before I'm 100 percent again."

Jamie was furious. "Are you kidding me?" she shouted. "How could you be so careless?"

"Enough!" the Duke shouted over the two, shutting them both up.

His rude explosion didn't sit well with Trinity. "You can't talk to us like that!" she said. "Who do you think you are?"

But before anyone could say another word, *swooop!* A large shadow flew swiftly over the village. Things were about to get a lot worse—for all of them.

Everyone looked up. An eerie and uncomfortable silence set in, much like the silence before. Seconds later …

Swooop! The shadow flew over the village a second time. The Duke and his men were no longer focused on the newcomers.

"Dragon!" shouted one of the Duke's men.

"Dragon!" shouted another, and then another and another after that.

Martha looked up. She didn't see anything in the sky, *especially a dragon.*

Trinity rolled her eyes at the men and muttered, "Dragons aren't real. *Losers.*"

Martha heard her mutter. "Dragons are very real," she assured her.

"Yeah, OK." Trinity scoffed. "Whatever you say, Grandma."

But the men shaking in their boots seemed to think the threat was real indeed. Soon, each and every one of the Duke's men were shouting, "Dragon!" They all trembled with fear, scattering on their horses as they rode the muddy path swiftly out of the village and over the hill until they were out of sight.

The Duke, however, was unafraid. But he knew he stood a better chance in battle if he wasn't alone. Though he fled, he swore to return with more men than before—this time with an army.

CHAPTER EIGHT
PEANUT BUTTER

As soon as the Duke and his band of thugs and thieves were gone, the large shadow in the sky suddenly seemed to vanish. It was the strangest thing.

Then, one of the women tied to the post struggled to speak, addressing Martha and her family. "My name is Gretchen," she said, her voice trembling. "This is my sister, Philine." Philine appeared to be the same age as Trinity. "She doesn't speak," Gretchen added.

Philine smiled through her fear and nodded, trying to wave with her hands tied behind her back. Both women were terrified and in tears.

Lucas and Trinity waved back. Jamie nudged them to stop.

"What, Mom?" Trinity asked, pulling out her phone and inconsiderately snapping a quick photo of the two women. "They're tied up. It's not like they're going to bite us."

"Put your phone away!" Jamie said, with a

furious look on her face, like she couldn't believe she'd even think about pulling it out again after that last encounter she'd had.

Lucas laughed at his sister getting scolded for her daftness, which didn't sit well with her.

"What are *you* laughing at?" Trinity exploded. "This is all *your* fault. We wouldn't even be in this mess if you weren't such a spazoid!"

"That's enough!" Jamie shouted. "What have I told you about using that word? Leave your brother alone. If you don't have anything nice to say, don't say anything at all."

"Seriously?" Trinity said, throwing her hands in the air. "You're defending him? That's so unfair!"

"We can worry about what's fair after we get the fu—udge out of here," Jamie said.

"Fudge? You brought fudge?" Martha asked, knowing full well that Jamie only used that word to cover up her almost slip-of-the-tongue, potty mouth.

"Don't be ridiculous," Jamie said. "No, I didn't bring any fudge. Now can we please go? Do I need to remind everyone that we're not in Kansas anymore?"

"Of course, we're not in Kansas," Martha said. "We never were. Ha! Read a map."

"Really, Ma?" Jamie huffed.

Lucas laughed at his grandmother's sarcasm. Trinity wanted to laugh, too but didn't.

"Don't encourage her," Jamie said with frustration.

"Please untie us!" Gretchen pleaded. *Sniff, sniff.* She sniffled and cleared her throat. "Please! I assure you, we mean you no harm."

Martha, *being Martha*, didn't hesitate for a single second in offering the stranger assistance.

"Of course, I'll untie you," she said as she lifted her drabby rags by the knee, left the porch, and walked with a pep in her step toward the women. She was most unusual to Gretchen and Philine, but her kindness put them at ease.

"What'd you get tied up for anyway?" Martha asked as she approached them. "If you don't mind my prying. What'd you do? Huh? Something naughty?"

"No, we did nothing of the sort," Gretchen answered humbly.

Philine shook her head, agreeing with her sister.

"We were simply walking across the bridge, heading to the castle to sell berries that we gathered near the forest when we were both suddenly attacked. The big man on the horse, *the same man you encountered yourself*, stopped us and demanded we hand over our berries for him and his men. He took the berries by force when I refused and punished us to this post."

"Well, *that's* not fair," Martha said, upset by how that lug had treated these two women. "But don't worry, all that is over now," she smiled. "And I'll have you free in a whiffy of a jiffy."

Gretchen looked at Philine, confused by the way Martha talked. Philine was just as confused. They didn't know what a "whiffy" or a "jiffy" was. But neither Gretchen nor Philine focused on Martha's behavior or how she talked. They were oh so happy and thankful to receive help from this oddball stranger.

Martha knew she had a knife or a pair of scissors inside her house that would cut the rope easily, which would've been much simpler than trying to untie it. It was a thick rope. But there was no time to go searching. Finding anything in that mess could take hours, and she had other problems to attend to—*like finding her broom and getting back home*. So she decided to look elsewhere. Martha knew she probably had something of use or at least something sharp hiding inside her hair that could also help. Her magical gas tank may have been empty for the time being, but she was always able to pull something whacky out of that wild hair of hers. So she reached in, hoping to find something to cut the rope, and ironically pulled out a laminated instructional pamphlet on knots instead.

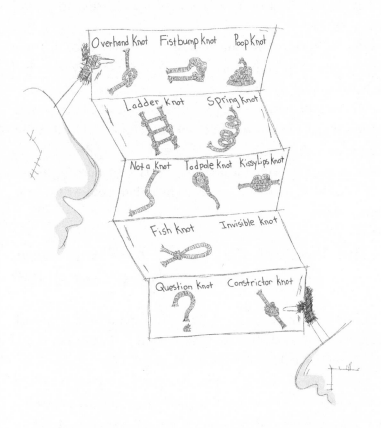

"Huh," Martha said, humored by the surprise. "What are the chances?" Even *she* wasn't expecting to pull out a pamphlet on knots. "Guess this will have to do."

Gretchen and Philine looked at each other and shrugged. They weren't even going to pretend to understand what was going on. They only wanted to be freed.

Martha held the pamphlet next to Gretchen's knot, trying to identify it. And there it was! "Aha!" she said, pointing to a specific knot. "Just as I thought. It's a simple overhand knot."

Martha was able to untie the knot with ease. With a quick loopy-loop here and a loopy-loop there, Gretchen was free. Gretchen rubbed her wrists with relief as she stood and then tried to free her sister.

Now Martha held the pamphlet next to Philine's knot, this time with concern. "Oh, cinnamon sticks," she said as her eyes reached the bottom of the pamphlet.

Philine's knot was much more complex. Her hands were bound using a constrictor knot, one of the most difficult knots to untie once secured. Martha and Gretchen struggled, trying to loosen it, but they were unsuccessful. This knot wouldn't loosen the slightest. If anything, it was tighter than before. To make matters worse …

The dragon was back! And this time, Martha saw it with her own eyes. They all did!

Jamie and the kids screamed, frightful and ready to run back inside the house. Martha braced herself, preparing for the worst, feeling helpless and afraid without her magic.

Luckily, she wouldn't need magic. This dragon wasn't a threat to her or anyone else for that matter—because it wasn't a dragon at all. It was something different, something totally unexpected, *more so* than a dragon. And it was heading toward the ground, to the exact spot where Martha was standing—like it was drawn to her.

As it slowly flew closer and closer, the fog surrounding the village disappeared, and this creature transformed midair, completely changing its appearance and even shrinking in size. It went from giant dragon to something else entirely in a matter of seconds. Once it landed on the ground, it revealed its true form, which was far less frightening and much, much smaller than it had appeared in the sky.

This creature was teensy-weensy, soft, and squishy too. It stood on two stubby little legs, barely reaching as tall as Lucas's knee, and had two short arms hanging over its plump belly, with three chubby little fingers on each hand and three chubby little toes on each foot. Both its hands and feet looked like puffy cartoonish paws, *its entire body* covered in fluffy pink fur, like fresh spun cotton candy from a carnival. It had two small round ears on top of its head, two beady little black eyes resting above its flat, wet, puppy-like nose, a round, cotton ball-shaped tail on its bottom, and it waddled like a duck when it walked. Aside from possibly being the cutest thing anyone had ever seen, this creature also seemed super friendly, with its tiny smile that never disappeared. But most spectacular of all—it spoke!

"Herro," it murmured with a squeak, waving its furry, three-fingered hand.

"No way!" Lucas shouted.

He and Trinity both smiled and waved back.

"Incredible!" Gretchen said, looking at the creature while still struggling to untie her sister. "It cannot be!"

"What is it?" Martha asked, picking up the creature to study. She lifted it high and curiously searched it with her hands as if looking for the battery compartment of a new toy. The creature didn't seem to mind either. It wiggled and giggled as her fingers tickled its fur.

"That's a mok," Gretchen said like she couldn't believe what she was seeing. "It must be."

"What's a mok?" Martha asked, lowering the creature close to her chest and coddling it like a newborn baby. "I've never heard of them."

"Moks are ancient, magical creatures," Gretchen explained. "Only, we've never seen one before."

"Up in the sky, though," Martha said, *puzzled*, "it looked like a giant dragon. *We all saw it.*"

"Oh yes," Gretchen continued. "Moks are able to take many forms. They are masters of illusion. From a distance, they can make you see whatever they want you to see, often something frightful and ferocious, though they are the kindest of creatures in all existence. They would never harm a soul. They only take these frightening forms to protect themselves by scaring away threatening predators before they get too close. A mok is also capable of detecting whether a person is good or evil and can sense when there is magic near. Perhaps you are the reason it appeared."

"Awww," Martha cooed, calling her grandchildren over for a closer look. "You gotta see this!" she shouted.

Lucas and Trinity jumped off the porch and ran to join their grandmother.

"You were helping us, weren't you, little guy?" Lucas asked.

The mok smiled and nodded yes. Then it took a deep breath, puffing up like a balloon, and floated in the air.

"So that's how you fly!" Martha said, astonished. "Extraordinary!"

"This is so cool," Lucas said. "It looks exactly like Baxter, the teddy bear I had when I was five. But Baxter was blue— *and a boy*. Is it a boy or a girl, Grandma?"

Martha was unsure. "Good question," she said. She grabbed the creature once more and looked closely at its undercarriage, unable to determine.

Lucas laughed. Again, Trinity wanted to laugh but didn't.

"Moks are neither male nor female," Gretchen informed.

"That makes sense, I guess," Martha said.

"How does that make sense?" Trinity asked rudely. "She's never even seen one. So what makes her an expert?"

Martha shoved Trinity with her elbow. "Don't be rude," she said.

"Yeah, because manners are what's important right now," Trinity replied sarcastically as she pulled out her phone and snapped a quick photo of the creature.

"Manners are always important," Martha reminded her. "Kindness is key. Now apologize. Right now!"

Trinity did as her grandmother said and offered Gretchen an apology—an obviously insincere apology. *"Sooooo sorry for being rude."*

Martha looked at Trinity—*really looked at her*—giving her the grandma staredown. Trinity knew that look too. It was the same look her mom gave her—*all the time.* She quickly realized how she was behaving toward these two women who had never done anything wrong to her and felt bad. So she offered a sincere apology this time. "I'm sorry," she said.

"No need to apologize," Gretchen said with grace. She looked at her sister, and they smiled at each other. "Our mother often told us stories when we were children. She told us many fascinating and wonderful things about moks. She would tell us how they would shed their fur but once every hundred years and how *that fur* would grow into a magical plant that would spawn the next generation of their kind. She believed moks to be the first creatures able to wield true magic, saying they were born from magic itself. But, of course, we thought her stories were merely bedtime tales to help us fall asleep. We never believed them to be true."

The mok floated over to Lucas and snuggled into his arms, purring like a giant pink kitten.

"Be careful!" Jamie shouted from the porch as she held on to her towel. "It could have rabies!"

Martha shook her head and disagreed, rolling her eyes so dramatically that it looked like she was trying to paint a rainbow with her eyeballs. "It doesn't," she said, or so she hoped.

"Can I name it, Grandma?" Lucas asked.

"I think that's a fabulous idea!" she answered. She looked at the mok and booped it on the nose with her finger. "Why, you deserve the best name ever, and there's no one better to name you than my grandson, Lucas."

So Lucas thought of a name, really thought hard, racking his brain, wondering what it should be. He wanted to come up with the absolute best name possible. Then he turned and looked at his sister, remembering how much she and Dad used to snack on peanut butter together, something Lucas had never had a taste for. He felt like a dog every time he tried to stomach even a spoonful of the sticky brown paste, which would cling to the roof of his mouth like superglue. Only for him, there was no satisfaction in trying to remove it with his tongue. He absolutely hated the stuff. But he thought it would make Trinity happy—he thought it would be the perfect name. "I'll call you ...Peanut Butter," he said as he rubbed its furry belly.

"Really?" Trinity said with a sour face. "That's a stupid name!"

Lucas hadn't expected her to react as she did, which made him sad. It was quite a shock.

But the mok didn't seem to think it was stupid. It purred with a smile. *Purrr.* It liked its new name.

Martha had just about *had it* with Trinity's attitude. She could tell that Lucas was trying to do something nice for his sister, and her reaction wasn't fair to him. So this time, Martha didn't waste any energy in giving her a grandma look. Instead, she went old-school witch in her approach to provide Trinity with a proper attitude adjustment. She pulled a loaf of fluffy white bread, *the good stuff*, from her hair and flung it at her granddaughter with all her might, hitting her in the face. *Smack!*

"*Ouuuch!* Seriously, Grandma?" Trinity shouted. But it didn't hurt. It was only soft bread. She was more embarrassed than anything.

"Don't be so mean to your brother!" Martha scolded. "You owe him an apology, *a real apology*. Next time, I won't throw bread. I'll make *mushrooms* grow between your toes!"

Martha widened her glare, pointing two fingers at her own eyes and then toward Trinity. She did that back and forth a few times, letting her know she meant business.

Again, Trinity realized how she was behaving and felt bad. Also, she didn't want mushrooms growing between her toes, and she knew her grandmother wasn't bluffing. "I'm sorry," she told Lucas. And she meant it. "Peanut Butter is a cool name."

"Thanks," Lucas said, who never held a grudge. "It's your favorite snack. Or it used to be. That's why I thought it would be the perfect name."

"Thanks," she said with a smile, placing her arm around him and scratching his head playfully, as she often would before their dad had died and they'd drifted apart.

Martha's quick-on-the-toes plan of bread-whooping her granddaughter worked brilliantly. Lucas and Trinity looked happy and seemed to be getting along for the first time in three months. But as luck would have it, this rekindling moment would have to wait. Because just when things seemed to be getting better . . .

The ground suddenly began to shake!

CHAPTER NINE
NO ESCAPE

Off in the distance, but not too far away, a loud sound could be heard over the hill, like a stampede of buffalo, and it was getting closer. The earth itself felt like it was moving. The frightened villagers continued to hide in their huts.

"What now?" Jamie huffed.

"I don't know," Martha said, her witch senses tingling like crazy. "But I have a bad feeling."

Martha grabbed Peanut Butter from Lucas and placed the furry creature on her shoulders. Reaching into her hair, she pulled out an old, rusty, antique telescope and a fresh new eye patch. She quickly placed the eye patch over one eye and looked through the telescope lens with the other. She looked far and wide but didn't see anything.

Lucas closed one eye and hooked his finger. "Arg," he said and chuckled.

Martha realized how she must have looked, wearing an eye patch and holding a telescope the way she was, so she joined in on the joke. She scrunched her face like the scurvy-ridden sea dweller Lucas was imagining her to be, hooked her finger the same way, and belted loudly, "Arg!" She and Lucas shared the same silly sense of humor, though right now was no time to joke around. Something was coming! But what? Maybe Jamie would have a better view since she stood higher on the porch.

"Here!" Martha said to Jamie. "Catch!" She threw the telescope.

Jamie caught it, almost losing her towel doing so.

"What do you see?" Martha asked.

Jamie looked through the telescope, searching the distance. At first, she didn't see anything either. "There's nothing there!" she said.

But Martha insisted, "Keep looking."

So Jamie continued looking through the telescope. But all she saw was grass and clouds and trees. There was nothing noticeable that could make such a loud noise. Still, she kept a sharp eye, searching side to side. Then, she saw them one by one as they crossed over the hilltop. She couldn't count them all. There were so many!

"Soldiers!" she shouted. "Hundreds of them!"

And they were being led by none other than—the Duke! He was returning to the village, as he swore he would.

This time, he didn't bring thugs or thieves. Instead, he brought warriors, elite warriors on horseback who were skilled in battle. He was returning with every soldier from the King's Guard. They rode fast, and they rode hard.

Now, nothing was going to stand in the Duke's way!

"We need to go!" Martha said to Gretchen with haste.

"I cannot leave my sister!" Gretchen replied. *"I will not!"*

Martha snapped her fingers a bunch, *snap, snap, snap, snap, snap,* trying to summon any bit of magic she may have had left. But it was no good. She was bone dry. "Oh, cinnamon sticks!"

Peanut Butter jumped off her shoulders and floated over to Philine to help with the knot. Peanut Butter tried and tried but was unsuccessful. The knot was too tough for this creature's furry little paws.

And there was no more time.

"They're here!" Jamie shouted. She tossed the telescope down and quickly ran to her kids.

Martha grabbed and then shoved Peanut Butter into her hair. Peanut Butter stayed hidden, peeking from behind her curls.

As the soldiers approached, covered in armor, they surrounded the entire village, forming an impenetrable blockade.

No one was going anywhere.

The Duke rode ahead. "Ha ha ha!" He laughed sinisterly, pulling back on the reins as he neared. "I said I would return. Here I am."

Wasting no time, he drew a wooden crossbow with notches marked into the wood and pointed it at Gretchen, who courageously stood before her sister, using her body as protection.

The Duke laughed again. "Ha ha ha! You cannot save her. You cannot save *yourself.* This day, you will both fall by my arrow. Like all the rest." He looked at the notches on his crossbow—then back at Gretchen and her sister. "There is no escape!"

The Duke turned to the soldiers. "We will kill the sisters first!" he yelled. "Then the witches! *All* of them," he added, looking directly at Trinity, letting her know he hadn't forgotten about her—or her magic black box. "*Then* we will slay the dragon!" He wore a wicked grin, licking his lips and savoring the satisfaction of what was soon to come—*death and slaughter.*

That was the moment when the Duke noticed the silence. *It is strangely quiet,* he thought as he trotted in a circle. He kept his arrow aimed at Gretchen as he struggled against his own armor to look up in search of the dragon. The sky was empty. There *was* no dragon. The way the Duke had explained the situation, the soldiers expected to arrive and see the greatest threat ever, as the Duke had never before retreated from any foe. But this was not the case.

The soldiers looked at each other and whispered among themselves. The Duke could hear them questioning whether or not he was telling the truth. They doubted there was ever a dragon, to begin with.

This infuriated the Duke! He refused to be made a fool of. So, without a dragon to slay, he unleashed his fury and anger on the sisters, the "witches," *and the entire village.*

"Sorcery!" he shouted. "These worthless peasants are aligned with the beast. That is why they dare not show themselves. They must be using magic to control it! Witches! All of them! Witches! We must cleanse this village! Then the beast is certain to show itself."

The Duke commanded the soldiers to kill every last person—men, women, and children alike. He wanted to decimate the entire village and turn it into a graveyard.

Many of the soldiers were conflicted with the order, but they readied their weapons for attack, prepared to do as they were told.

Lucas and Trinity were terrified. They held each other close as they stood with their mom.

Martha tried to think of a way to help Gretchen and Philine *and* save her family. But it was too late.

The Duke attacked!

He released an arrow from his crossbow, flying with great speed—straight toward Gretchen. There was nothing she could do but watch as the sharp silver tip of the arrow that would soon pierce her flesh soared toward her.

"I'm sorry," she whispered to her sister as a final teardrop rolled down her cheek. She closed her eyes and braced herself.

But just before the Duke's arrow struck Gretchen, a mysterious warrior woman appeared from nowhere!

In a display of great speed and strength, she jumped in front of Gretchen and caught the arrow with her bare hand. With a simple flick of her wrist, she snapped the arrow in half. *Snap!* She then used the tip of the arrow to free Philine, swiftly slashing the rope that bound her—*in a single pass.*

Who was this mysterious warrior woman? No one knew. But whoever she was, she was unlike anyone else. She stood tall and strong, *beautiful*, although filthy and unkempt, with fiery red hair braided thick as rope whipping down her back—her skin shielded in dried mud and wrapped in layers of leaves and vines.

Every one of the soldiers stared at this strange and majestic-looking woman, captivated by her bewitching beauty and daring rescue. Her presence alone was enough to catch the eyes of even the Duke himself—*that is*—until she opened her mouth and spoke. She stared at the Duke with boiling rage and wailed out ...

"Mahahahaha!"

After that, those who found her to be mysterious or majestic—instead—suddenly thought *she must be a raving lunatic.*

They all stared in silence—all but one.

Martha's jaw dropped open, and she shouted, **"Bubbles?"**

She lifted her eye patch with surprise and excitement and then slammed it back down with an explosive laugh, shifting it to the other eye. She couldn't believe it! "Bu-bu-bu-but how?" she blurted.

CHAPTER TEN

THE COUNCIL
AND THE CURSE

Trinity pulled out her phone and snapped a quick photo of the warrior woman.

Jamie didn't know why on earth her mom was babbling about her goat. Had she completely lost her mind? "Ma!" she shouted. "That's not your stupid goat!" She thought her mom was having a stroke. But Jamie was wrong—*dead wrong.*

This warrior woman was indeed Bubbles!

Remember the yellow shower? Bubbles had still been on top of the roof of Martha's house when Lucas had eaten his grandmother's slice of magical cake and unknowingly made a wish. Before she'd had a chance to get down, the house had lifted, and she, too, had traveled back in time. Seconds before the house landed, though, she had been *flung* from the roof. Somehow, she'd miraculously landed in the exact same spot as Martha and her family, only she had landed there five years earlier—*no longer a goat*. But then again, Bubbles was never really a goat, to begin with. Believe it or not—Martha wasn't lying when she told Lucas Bubbles was magical. As a matter of fact, not only was Bubbles magical, but she was also once a witch herself—*a mighty strong, and beautiful witch*.

A long time ago, Bubbles was known far and wide—as Jezebel. But she wasn't known solely for her beauty or strength back then. She was particularly known for something else entirely—*her magic*—and the women she practiced magic *with*. Jezebel belonged to an ancient and elite sisterhood of witches, who were *also* known far and wide for their magic as well. But Jezebel and these other witches were not only known; *they were feared*. For in this group of women were some of the most powerful and dangerous witches in all existence. They called themselves …

The Council.

The Council was led by a master witch named Lady Bishop, the most notorious and powerful of them all. She was one of the oldest and most ruthless witches alive. Under her guidance, the Council practiced every form of magic known and even experimented with creating their own. Together, the Council combined their powers, pushing magic to its limit. They knew no bounds. Their powers were endless.

The Council was behind some of the most catastrophic events throughout history—carelessly tipping the scales of balance and tempting fate. They were like a scourge upon the earth, responsible for more than 50 percent of the world's war, famine, and disease. They even had a hand in the majority of the world's everyday seemingly insignificant inconveniences, such as clogged toilets, stubbed toes, and pets that refused to potty train. These were just a few of the small things they'd conjure up during their downtime. They craved chaos and had no regard for *anyone* or *anything*. They willingly sacrificed *all* in the pursuit of power.

Now, the witches in the Council weren't always evil. These women had once been ordinary people—mothers, daughters, and sisters—who'd sadly become corrupted and consumed by magic, each of them depending on the other for their magic to stay strong. But, even though they were corrupt, they shared a bond that had never before been broken.

The Council dedicated themselves to the practice of magic. Magic was everything to them. Without it, there was no purpose to life. Needless to say, they took it rather seriously. They were constantly, day after day, night after night, conjuring up new, never-before-used spells and mixing all sorts of different potions. After all, ruining the world takes a lot of hard work. Being evil isn't easy, no matter how easy it looks. However, when you possess the sort of powers these witches possessed, and you've seen and done the things they had, a Monday-through-Sunday routine can become a bit … mundane. They were bored—bored out of their witching minds! They needed something to lift them out of their funk and add excitement back into their lives. Thankfully …

They had poker!

It was the only thing they took more seriously than magic. The Council was notorious for gambling. They loved it! Nothing excited them more than the fresh smell of a new deck of cards being shuffled. The flapping sound of the fifty-two cards smacking together was magic in itself! So they came together every Tuesday night at precisely seven o'clock for a game of five-card draw, Jokers wild. And boy, did they look forward to it. They played game after game into the late hours of the night, laughing and joking and sharing stories about the lives they ruined each day. But they didn't gamble for money. No. No. No. "Who needs paper or coin?" they'd say. They loved the corruption that it caused, but money meant *nothing* to them. They played against each other for something far more precious and desirable.

They played for potions and spells.

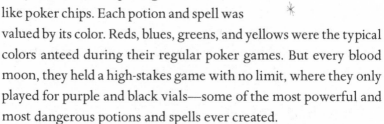

You see, each witch in the Council possessed a certain amount of magic not shared with the others. This magic is how they kept poker night interesting. With the magic they retained for themselves, they created their own individual potions and spells, each unique for their different capabilities. They bottled them up and gambled them like poker chips. Each potion and spell was valued by its color. Reds, blues, greens, and yellows were the typical colors anteed during their regular poker games. But every blood moon, they held a high-stakes game with no limit, where they only played for purple and black vials—some of the most powerful and most dangerous potions and spells ever created.

During one of those high-stakes games, Jezebel got greedy. A witch by the name of Ruby Redenbacher went all in with a black potion unlike any before, capable of transforming even the most powerful witch *into a goat*! And once transformed, she could never change back.

Jezebel wanted that potion. But she knew she didn't stand a chance at winning fair and square because she had been dealt a pair of twos, with an eight as her high card—a very weak hand. Still, she was determined to beat Ruby at any cost.

So she cheated!

Using her magic, Jezebel changed her cards into a winning hand—*which was a very bad move.* How foolish—to think she could cheat against the Council and not get caught. This move was especially foolish—because these particular cards belonged to none other than Lady Bishop herself—and were unknowingly protected by her magic. Any witch who even *thought* about cheating was in for an embarrassing surprise. Because that witch, without warning, would be exposed to all at the table and labeled right there on the spot as a big, fat, no-good cheater by Lady Bishop's hiccup-till-it-hurts spell. As its name suggested, this spell caused sudden and extreme hiccups until it hurt.

But these were no ordinary hiccups.

Lady Bishop had a dark sense of humor like no other. Her hiccup-till-it-hurts spell caused the cheater to hiccup uncontrollably until bubbles came spewing out of her mouth, one right after the other, *nonstop*. The spell didn't stop there, either. The bubbles spoke! Each bubble would float until it popped, and with each pop, it would shout, "Cheater!" If the cheater tried to cover her mouth to hide the fact that she'd been caught, the bubbles then came spewing out of her nose, her ears, and even her bottom, hundreds of them! *Pop! Pop! Pop!* "Cheater! Cheater! Cheater!" Once again, it was *very* embarrassing. There was no way to cheat without getting caught, not with that many bubbles.

The rules were simple. Any witch who cheated at poker was automatically disqualified from the game and no longer allowed to be a member of the Council. So Jezebel was cast out, abandoned by her own for not upholding the sanctity of poker night. The bond that had never been broken—had now been shattered.

All in the Council would have been satisfied simply with casting Jezebel out—except Ruby Redenbacher, who was furious! She demanded more be done. She wanted to exact her *own* vengeful justice, and after a quick deliberation, the Council agreed to her demands.

"Do as you will," they said, giving the matter no more thought.

And with their permission, Ruby did just that.

Jezebel was forced to drink Ruby Redenbacher's potion and was transformed into a goat. The very potion she'd tried to steal became her curse. She felt like an idiot, and, *worse*, soon became the laughingstock of the entire witch community. As the news spread about her expulsion, no witch ever spoke to her again.

Ruby still wasn't satisfied, though. It wasn't enough for her to turn Jezebel into a goat and take away everything she held dear. She had always been jealous of Jezebel's beauty. For that reason alone, she'd never liked her and wanted her to suffer—*really suffer*. But even as a goat, Jezebel could still be quite beautiful. What if she was the most beautiful goat anyone had ever seen? The thought alone was enough to infuriate Ruby. So she did her worst and made some last-minute changes to her potion before it was consumed, not only turning Jezebel into a goat but rendering her hairless and nearly blind, with leaky udders and disfigured horns and hooves. She really let her have it! She warped Jezebel's body from head to toe with grotesque deformities, ridding her of any beauty she'd once possessed. People she would soon encounter only saw a monster, and they treated her like one too. It was Ruby's final and cruel sense of justice.

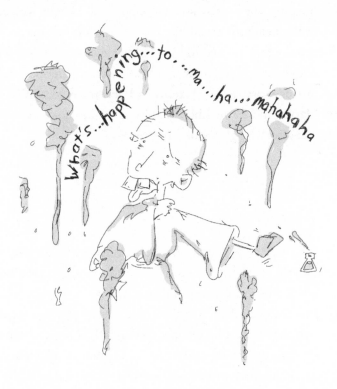

It wasn't long before Jezebel's magic grew weak. For many years, she'd been accustomed to the combined power of the Council, so she'd forgotten what it was like to wield magic all on her own. She eventually found herself unable to conjure even the simplest spell and was forced to roam in search of a new home—*on hooves*!

Jezebel wandered aimlessly. She walked about as a lonely goat for years, with only her thoughts and repulsive stench to keep her company. Then one night, by chance, under a starry Texas sky, she crossed paths with none other than Martha May McKenzie, who just so happened to be a witch and, believe it or not, spoke fluent goat.

Upon meeting Jezebel, Martha knew there was more than meets the eye when it came to this goat. The two quickly became close, forming their own strong bond, and Martha vowed to help her. Jezebel didn't smell like rot, dog vomit, or papaya in the slightest bit, which proved to Martha that she wasn't a bad witch, just a fellow sister of magic who'd lost her way. After hearing the embarrassing story of how Jezebel had become a goat in the first place, Martha nicknamed her Bubbles, and the name just sort of stuck. They both laugh about it to this day.

Now, after Lucas's wish sent Bubbles traveling back in time, somehow, the curse had been lifted. Bubbles was finally herself once again, free from those hideous horns, heavy hooves, and loathsome leaky udders. She also didn't have any use for those clunky glasses Martha had made. Her sight had been restored, as well as her strength and beauty. She could finally walk on her own two feet, no longer a goat—well, sort of. Unfortunately, she still sounded like one whenever she tried to speak and was still unable to use her magic. And for the past five years, she'd been hiding in the forest all alone.

Fortunately, Martha's wonky broom had landed with Bubbles, which had certainly helped her survive in this timeline that was quite different from her own. She'd tried to use the broom to return to her own timeline but was unable to do so. She didn't have the ability to wield the broom the same as Martha. Even if she could, she didn't know if the broom was powerful enough to handle such a stretch of unmeasurable distance. As a result, Bubbles was limited to traveling small distances. Instead, she used the broom to remain hidden and unseen.

In fact, because of Bubbles, the villagers thought the forest was haunted. Bubbles was a deep, *deep* sleeper, often snoring and talking in her sleep, and sometimes she even yelled and moaned. So when they began to hear loud goat noises coming from beyond the trees at night, only ever seeing glimpses of what looked like a tall, vanishing figure, they thought a demon creature had possessed the forest—but it was only Bubbles.

Now, after waiting five long years, Bubbles was more than ready to get home—even if it meant the spell she was finally free from could possibly return, and she'd be a goat once more. She didn't care. But because she'd used the broom so much already, only a handful of bristles remained. She knew Martha was her only chance back home, and she wasn't about to let a giant oaf on a horse steal that chance away from her.

CHAPTER ELEVEN

THE SCREAMING FOREST

After Bubbles effortlessly caught and snapped the Duke's arrow, she held the broken pieces in her hand and stood defiant before his entire army. She was fearless! She dropped the broken pieces to the ground and stomped them into the dirt with her bare feet.

She looked at the Duke, whose anger and fury only grew stronger, and curled her lip into a smile. "Mahahahaha," she bleated, laughing loudly, which in goat meant, "Is that the best you can do? I think you gave me a splinter."

"Haha. Good one," Martha chuckled.

But the Duke didn't understand a word Bubbles was saying. No one did. After all, Martha was the only one there who spoke any goat.

"Enough!" the Duke shouted. He refused to be made a fool

of any further. He demanded immediate retribution for his embarrassment!

He wanted blood!

In a desperate attempt to rid the land of the wretched witches that stood before him, the Duke commanded every soldier with a crossbow to rain down arrows over the entire village.

"Let's see you catch these," he whispered with an evil smirk, quickly reloading his *own* crossbow.

As the soldiers pointed their arrows, Bubbles slowly backed away toward Martha. She put her hands up as if she had nowhere else to go and was ready to surrender.

The Duke turned to the soldiers and laughed. "Like a mouse cowering back to its hole!" he said.

But Martha knew better. Bubbles was no coward. Martha knew she had a plan; she just didn't know *what* that plan was. Then Martha noticed her wonky broom entangled in Bubbles's braided hair, concealed behind her back, and her eyes lit up. That's when the plan became clear to her.

Once Bubbles was within arm's reach, Martha quickly grabbed her broom. "Everyone!" she shouted. "Latch on to me as if your life depended on it. And no matter what, don't let go! *Quickly now.*"

No one questioned her or hesitated in doing what she said. Their reaction was flawless. Trinity and Lucas grabbed her ankles, Gretchen and Philine grabbed her arms, Jamie and Bubbles grabbed her wrists, and Peanut Butter simply stayed put, gripping Martha's curls.

The Duke had a hunch they would soon try to escape, and he wasn't about to let them slip his grasp.

"Now!" he shouted, firing the first shot.
"Release your arrows!"

The soldiers followed the Duke's command, and they all released at the same time. *Phew! Phew! Phew! Phew! Phew!* Hundreds of arrows cut through the sky as they soared toward the village. The villagers would be safe, *for now*, as long as they stayed shielded in their huts.

Martha and the others, however, would certainly meet their doom if they stood there for even a moment longer. *The arrows were seconds away from striking.* Martha looked over at the forest. *They'll never find us in there*, she thought. She closed her eyes and scrunched her face, concentrating her thoughts on the forest—then quickly plucked a bristle from her broom just before the arrows struck. And—*poof!*—they magically disappeared in a purple puff of smoke.

Seconds later—*poof!*—they magically reappeared in a blue puff of smoke safely in the forest. They had narrowly escaped.

"Everyone OK?" Martha asked as she unscrunched her face and opened her eyes.

"Mahahahaha," Bubbles bleated, which meant, "Yes."

"I believe we are," Gretchen said, checking on her sister.

Philine nodded.

"Herro," Peanut Butter murmured with a squeak, still hidden in Martha's hair.

Jamie didn't answer. She couldn't. Her hand was covering her mouth, and her face was sickly green. She quickly turned around and barfed chunks all over the ground. Her vomit splattered everywhere, and it smelled rancid.

"Eww." Martha cringed. Covering her nose, she reached into her hair and pulled out a travel-size lemon-scented spray. She sprayed all around Jamie's face, spraying and spraying and spraying, even after spraying some in her eyes and mouth, still spraying and spraying and spraying, emptying the bottle completely before stuffing it back inside her hair.

"OK, OK!" Jamie said, coughing. *Cough. Cough. Cough.* "Enough already!"

Martha also pulled out a napkin and tossed it to Jamie so she could wipe the barf from around her mouth. The napkin magically disappeared as soon as she had finished wiping.

"Remind me never to do that again," Jamie said, trying to laugh it off. Then she felt Trinity's shaky hand softly tap against her skin.

"Um, Mmm-Mmm-Mom," Trinity stammered, uneasy and afraid, rattled to her core and trembling. Jamie knew by her daughter's tone that something awful had happened. She turned to look. *Gasp!* Jamie's entire body fell numb from shock. She couldn't believe her eyes.

Not everyone had escaped unharmed.

Lucas was lying motionless on the ground. One arrow—*the Duke's arrow*—had made it through before they'd all disappeared to the forest.

And it had struck Lucas in the heart.

"Lucas?" Jamie whispered. She reached out and touched his body. Her voice cracked. "Baby? Sweetheart? No. Oh no, no, no." Her hands began to shake. "No. This can't be happening."

Lucas didn't seem to be breathing.

"It's not possible," Jamie uttered. Her eyes became a pool of tears. "It's just not possible." She grabbed him by his limp shoulders and sat him up. She shook him. "Wake up!" she screamed. "Wake up!"

She shook him over and over again—so hard his glasses flung off his face—but it made no difference. Lucas didn't wake up.

"He's dead!" Jamie cried out. "He's dead!"

"Do something!" she begged her mom. "Use your magic!"

But there was nothing Martha could do. Magic or no magic, this was beyond her ability. Jamie wept over Lucas's body with a shattered heart. She cried and cried hysterically. Her tears hit the ground like stones. Jamie couldn't bear the loss; the unimaginable, agonizing pain and suffering, the worst conceivable kind, struck her like a bolt of lightning.

Consumed by her grief, she was quickly overtaken by anger and hatred. It filled her, poisoning her mind and awakening something evil inside her.

Jamie slowly raised her head in anger, furiously clenching her teeth. She furrowed her brow and pushed her fingers deep into the ground, burying them beneath the dirt. As she did so, she began to experience a *new* surge of pain, a horribly horrible *physical* pain—and it was coming on fast.

"What's happening to me?" she shouted, fearful but lost in her rage. Her lips quivered. "Ma?"

Her skin boiled and popped with bubbles, and waves of heat poured out of her profusely. Her stomach rolled and rumbled like a ferocious volcano, and her insides felt like molten lava as she continued to grow angry in her grief. Sweat evaporated as quickly as it ran down her face, and smoke seeped from her mouth as she panted heavily. This tormenting pain, however, was nothing compared to how she felt after losing her son. At first, it didn't 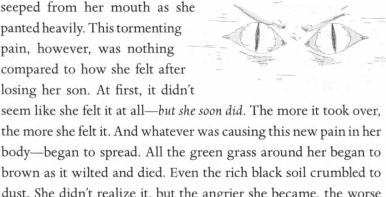 seem like she felt it at all—*but she soon did*. The more it took over, the more she felt it. And whatever was causing this new pain in her body—began to spread. All the green grass around her began to brown as it wilted and died. Even the rich black soil crumbled to dust. She didn't realize it, but the angrier she became, the worse things turned—*for everyone*. She closed her eyes—squeezing them shut—and when she opened them, they were no longer the same. She now had the eyes of a serpent, wild and green, and *her own sight* was completely gone. Everyone and everything around her seemed to fade—until all was unrecognizable.

But one person remained, one person she could still see, the one responsible—*the Duke*.

"Youuu!" Jamie howled savagely, staring past the trees at the Duke.

Jamie's voice was no longer her own. It was loud and powerful, and it shook the entire forest.

"Mom!" Trinity cried out in tears. "What's happening?"

But Jamie didn't respond. She had become completely unhinged.

Martha grabbed Trinity. "Stay behind me," she said as she watched in terror.

Jamie began to barbarically hammer the ground with her fists. She screamed and screamed as she pulverized the dirt.

Booooom! Booooom! Booooom!

The earth quaked with each blow.

Then, suddenly, a screeching wind swept through the forest, creating a wild whirling dust storm. With each pass, the wind grew stronger and stronger, bending the trees with its might while Jamie screamed and writhed in agony. Her screams burrowed in the ears of every person gathered near and far—but never reached the kingdom.

As the storm raged on, Martha and the others hunkered down as low as they could, trying to resist the force of the powerful wind. They held on to each other, forming a circle around Lucas's body.

Martha thought if Jamie could hear her voice, it might help to calm her. "Jamie!" she shouted. "Please, you need to calm down!"

But it was useless. Jamie heard nothing. Martha's voice was lost in the wind. There wasn't anything she could do to help Jamie now. Something sinister was happening, and it was beyond anyone's reach.

CHAPTER TWELVE

A SACRIFICE

Martha feared the worst was far from over. She also feared she may have had a hand in whatever dark forces were at play here. Of course, there was no way Martha could've known for sure. But deep down, she always felt a day like this would come, for what she and her husband, Harold, had done many years ago—when Jamie was just a child.

This was that day.

The moment Jamie came into this world was the happiest moment of her parents' lives. On that day, Harold had decided it would be best if Martha put away her witchy ways, and together, they would raise their daughter without the help of magic.

Though Martha had the ability to wield magic, her daughter hadn't inherited that ability. Jamie hadn't been born with any magical gifts whatsoever. She was born a happy, healthy, ordinary baby. But Martha and Harold knew there was still a chance Jamie could develop powers, so they watched her closely for the first couple of years to make sure.

Harold was no witch, but he knew all about Martha's special abilities. The two had known each other since they were children and never kept any secrets. Harold knew of the great wonders magic could bring, but he also knew of the dangers. As kids, Martha had once tried to remove a splinter from his hand using her magic, but she'd given him twenty more splinters instead—twice in size! His hand had looked like a pincushion and had been swollen for weeks after. Then, only a couple of days after that incident, Harold had complained about an upset stomach, and Martha had tried once more to heal him with her magic—and once more, it didn't go as planned. In her attempts to help Harold, Martha accidentally replaced his belly button with an eyeball—an actual functioning, seeing, blinking eyeball—*and it stayed on him for almost three whole days.* But that was a long time ago. Martha was young and inexperienced back then. Luckily, they were only splinters. No harm, no foul. And honestly, who couldn't use an extra eyeball for a few days? Still, mistakes when using magic could be much more serious and have *much, much* more severe consequences. So Martha had agreed. The two of them did just as they'd discussed and gave their daughter the most ordinary human life possible, and it was wonderful. But it only lasted a short while.

Soon, in all their happiness—tragedy struck!

On Jamie's third birthday, she became sick with an unknown illness. Doctors tried everything to heal her, but nothing worked. She was beyond the help of modern medicine and would most certainly die. But her dad refused to give up. Doctors may not have been able to help Jamie, but Harold knew there was still one last thing he and Martha could do to try to save their little girl, though it hadn't been practiced in a few years—*Martha's magic.*

Now, again, Martha was unable to bring anyone back from the dead. No witch had ever succeeded in doing that, though many had tried. However, she knew of a spell, one in particular, able to bring a person back from the *clutches* of death—where the dead aren't dead yet. The spell was known as—*Dead Man's Last Request*. If there was any chance to save their daughter, this was the spell that could do it.

There was only one problem.

It required dark magic, something Martha knew very little about. She only ever practiced good magic and used hers for conjuring lighthearted, mischievous spells meant for fun and simple problem-solving. She warned Harold of the terrible and sinister dangers involved with dabbling, even the slightest bit, in dark magic. If executed perfectly, there was still the possibility that the spell would not work.

But Harold was willing to take that chance. He insisted, regardless of the consequences! Any chance was a chance worth taking. And against everything wrong she knew could happen, Martha wanted this too. So she conjured the spell.

"Blood of my blood. My life. My breath. I call upon dark magic and humbly beg a Dead Man's Last Request—let my daughter live."

After, Harold had expected the spell to work instantly—but that's not what happened. Martha told him the spell could take some time. This form of magic was, after all, very unfamiliar to her. Even she, being a witch, didn't know what to expect. Worry set in after seconds turned into minutes, and nothing happened. Then, minutes turned into hours. Still—nothing. But what else could they do? This was their only hope. So, they worried and waited even longer. They worried and waited—and worried—and waited. For nine whole days, Martha and Harold anxiously worried and waited, holding onto the tiny flickering ember of hope they had left for even a glimmer of movement from Jamie's body. They didn't eat. They didn't sleep. They didn't so much as blink. They simply stayed put, worrying and waiting.

And finally, after worrying and waiting for so long—the spell worked!

Miraculously they had their daughter back. Jamie's illness vanished. She was healthier than ever and thriving amazingly. Martha and Harold were filled with relief and overwhelming joy!

Unfortunately, the feeling didn't last long. There was a price to pay for using dark magic—*a grave price*—beyond what any witch or mortal being would ever want to bargain for, and any who practiced dark magic paid that price every time. There was one who made certain of it. No good witch ever wanted to meet him. He was just a shadow of a man, the floating darkness of what once was and will never be again. He had no eyes to see, no mouth to speak, and no ears to listen, only shadowy hands—with creepy long fingers—to take what was his. He couldn't be reasoned with, and he offered no deals. He was neither good nor evil; he was the balance between the two—no more, no less.

He had no name, but those unfortunate enough to owe such a debt called him—the Collector.

You see, any time dark magic is used, whether, by a good witch or a bad witch, something almost always needs to be sacrificed, usually something of equal or greater value. And in Martha's case, it was the greatest sacrifice she would ever have to make—*a life for a life*. This rule was something she had been unaware of, though. She'd had no idea that, in saving Jamie's life, she'd be sacrificing Harold's; he was her one true love and the *only* love she had ever known before her daughter. But there was no turning back now. The magic was already in motion.

Sadly, each day Jamie grew stronger, Harold became weaker. As Jamie's color returned to her cheeks, Harold's faded. Jamie continued to get better, while Harold continued to get worse. Finally, Martha realized—Harold had taken on their daughter's illness, swapping fates with her entirely. Martha was in constant anguish and torment, watching her husband slowly wither away as their daughter continued to thrive, unable to grieve and unable to celebrate. Worst of all, Martha went through it alone.

On the day of his death, Harold made Martha swear she would never speak of what they had done to save their daughter. It was his dying wish for it to always remain a secret. "The past is the past," he whispered with his final breath. He didn't want his daughter to feel guilt or sadness when remembering him. He wanted her to grow up happy and enjoy life. He didn't care what happened to him if it meant her safety. He gladly sacrificed himself. Though it was a sad day for Martha and Jamie, Harold took comfort in knowing his daughter was alive and well and would still have her mother. He died with a smile, knowing he had helped save her.

But all was not as it should be. Martha's spell had another effect, one she could never have foreseen. Jamie, who was once ordinary, now carried dark magic inside her. And it remained inside her, dormant for many years, unstirred, but still present and very much alive, waiting for the chance to be free.

And now it was.

CHAPTER THIRTEEN

THE CHANGE

Deep in the forest, the wind continued to howl and bend the trees. All Martha could do was clench her teeth in terror and watch as the dark magic inside Jamie finally came to life and took hold of her. Under its grip, Jamie's body began to change—*rapidly and uncontrollably*—morphing into something unknown and menacing. The dark magic caused her to spiral out of control and go berserk!

Out of nowhere, she grabbed her jaw, violently jammed her hand into her mouth, and began yanking out her own teeth.

Trinity was horrified! She screamed and hid her frightened eyes against her grandmother as her mother continued pulling out tooth, after tooth, after tooth. With each tooth Jamie pulled, new teeth quickly grew. They were long, giant teeth, jagged and sharp. They ripped through her gums as they pushed through.

As Jamie's bizarre behavior went on, she scratched and clawed at her skin, scratching, and scratching, and scratching, digging her nails deeper and deeper with each pass. And when her nails could dig no further, she desperately pulled the flesh from her bones, layer by layer, with ease—finally unmasking the dark magic inside after all these years. Hiding beneath Jamie's mangled flesh were bright red scales, *hundreds of them,* each one stacked on top of the other, covering her entire body like armor. And if that wasn't bad enough …

Jamie began to grow in size. She grew tall, and she grew wide.

Her hands and feet became giant razor-sharp claws, and her spine stretched into a long tail riddled with spikes as hard as iron. With every movement, she swung her tail carelessly, whipping it wildly against the trees. The spikes tore through the trees with ease, snapping them like twigs. With each swing, she became bigger and bigger. She continued to grow, and it didn't seem like she'd ever stop.

Jamie grew and grew and grew—until finally—she stood taller than the forest itself, casting *her own* dark shadow of fear. Then, she reached her neck as high as it would go, staring straight up, and *roared* a fierce roar that thundered through the clouds. *Roooaaaarrrrr!*

But it wasn't over.

Just when her transformation seemed to be complete—she sprouted giant wings that spanned across the entire forest—*and she filled the sky with her fiery breath.*

Now, Jamie was truly lost. What the dark magic had festered into was all that

remained—pure evil incarnate, a monstrosity, a true nightmare come to life—a dragon! And this time, it was no illusion.

Outside the forest, the soldiers' horses were going wild with fear. The dragon's fiery roar was scratching at their ears. But it wasn't only the horses that were scared. The soldiers were afraid as well. They had never heard *anything like this* before. Some shouted that the forest was cursed and they'd be doomed if they entered. Out of fear, many pleaded with the Duke to turn around and head back to the castle.

But the Duke demanded they follow him into the forest, reminding them of the consequence should any of them choose otherwise. "Follow me!" he commanded. "Or face my blade!"

At that moment, the dragon lifted its wings high and, in a single flap, hoisted itself up into the air.

The soldiers couldn't believe their eyes as they saw the monster that emerged from deep within the forest. None of them had ever faced such an enormous and ferocious threat.

"Retreat! Back to the castle!" they screamed like scared children, ignoring and abandoning the Duke, who watched with anger as they fled.

"Cowards!" he shouted. "The whole lot of you! Cowards!"

All together, the soldiers rode away as fast as they could—except for the Duke, who showed no fear.

"At last, a challenge," he said, imagining his victorious battle. And he couldn't wait for his reward. He wanted this dragon's head!

But the dragon wanted his head as well, and it wasted no time in going after him.

With the Duke in sight, the dragon plunged toward him like a giant roaring missile, setting itself ablaze as it hurled his way.

This is it, the Duke thought, jumping off his horse. *Glory or death!* As he landed, he planted his feet firmly on the ground and slapped his horse on the rear. The horse let out a loud neigh as it took off running, kicking up dust as it quickly galloped away.

The Duke stood alone. He reloaded his crossbow as fast as he could and aimed high. He knew he only had one shot and had to make it count. So he waited patiently for the dragon to get within range—*then released his arrow.*

He watched with confidence as his arrow soared toward the dragon. He was certain this would be the fatal blow that would bring down the beast and deliver him glory. But in his arrogance, he was wrong. The arrow struck the dragon—*tink*—but shattered against its armor of scales. It didn't even leave a scratch.

The dragon was now too close for the Duke to reload another arrow, which had proved useless anyway. So he dropped the crossbow and grabbed his great big sword instead. He unsheathed it from his back—*shing!*—gripped it tightly with both hands, and prepared for the greatest battle of his life. But before he even had a chance to swing ...

Swooop! Chomp!

The dragon swooped down and gobbled him up, swallowing him whole, great big sword and all!

He never stood a chance. The battle was over before it had even begun. But, unfortunately, it wasn't finished. The dragon's appetite for destruction was insatiable, and it had now set its sights on something much bigger—*the castle!* Once again, it rose high into the sky, hiding behind the clouds, and followed the soldiers, who had no idea of the danger they were bringing back with them. Like a trail of breadcrumbs, they unknowingly led the way.

Meanwhile, the forest was collapsing. The dark magic overtaking Jamie had sucked its life force dry during her transformation—*bringing everything crumbling down.* Martha held Trinity close as Gretchen and Philine huddled next to her. She thought for sure they'd all be crushed by the falling trees.

She threw herself over Lucas's body, apologizing and begging for forgiveness. "I'm so sorry!" she cried. "This was never supposed to happen!" She grabbed Trinity's hand and gripped it tightly.

"I'm scared," Trinity cried. "I wanna go home!"

"I know," Martha said, assuring her she'd find a way to make that happen. But she knew the inevitable was near.

Just then, a giant tree big enough to crush an entire house began falling, and it was aimed to fall right on top of them!

This was it! Martha knew for certain they were done for.

"Mahahahaha!" Bubbles bleated, gesturing to Martha's broom, but there was no time. They all threw their hands over their heads, covering themselves as they hunched over and squeezed their eyes shut.

But not Martha. She still felt it was her duty to protect her grandchildren, even when all hope was lost, and it seemed impossible. She blindly flung her arm out in a desperate attempt to stop the tree, using her bare hand. It was foolish and crazy!

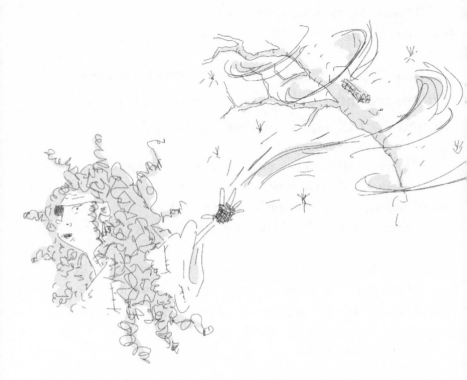

But to her surprise, it worked! They were unharmed—*and*—there was more. As soon as everyone opened their eyes, they saw the tree floating above them, just feet away, and Martha was somehow controlling it—which only meant one thing.

Her magic had returned.

This was great. Now there was a fighting chance.

And that wasn't all. There was also hope, especially for Jamie, because in that very moment—*Lucas opened his eyes!*

CHAPTER FOURTEEN

TO THE KINGDOM

Lucas sat straight up as if he was waking from a dreadful nightmare and took a deep breath.

"He's OK, Grandma!" Trinity called out. "He's alive!"

"*Lucas!*" Martha shouted, splendidly surprised. "My sweet boy! *You're alive!*" Unable to control her excitement, Martha tossed the floating tree aside like it was one of her red banana peels. It shook the ground as it landed, and everybody bounced up and down.

Martha grabbed Lucas and swallowed him in a great big clumsy hug.

He grunted in pain, gesturing to the giant arrow still lodged in his chest.

"Oh, my goodness. I'm so sorry!" she said, gently releasing him.

Trinity quickly helped Lucas find his glasses. Once she found them, she cleaned the lenses with her sleeve and gently placed them on his face. Then she, too, gave him a great big hug.

"I can't believe you're alive!" she said. She squeezed him tightly (minding the arrow, of course). "I love you so much! I'm so happy you're not dead!" But Trinity was still *Trinity*. She pulled out her phone and snapped a quick photo.

"Thanks, I guess," Lucas said, looking down, confused. He then gripped the arrow with both hands.

"Wait! What are you doing?" Martha asked with worry.

"It's OK, Grandma," he assured her. "I think I can just—" Lucas paused and bravely yanked the arrow from his chest with one forceful jerk. "Got it!"

To his grandmother's surprise, there wasn't a single drop of blood.

"What the cinnamon sticks?" Martha said, double-checking to make sure the arrow was real. She was so confused. She thought for certain it had pierced his heart. But it hadn't even pierced his skin. He had simply been knocked unconscious from the heavy blow.

"I don't understand," Martha said, her eyes fixed on the sharp pointy tip.

Lucas reached into his shirt, behind his suspender strap where the arrow had struck him, and pulled out one of Martha's "useless" eye patches, the very same one he'd picked up from the porch earlier.

"Your eyepatch saved me, Grandma," he said with a grin.

"But how?"

He reached out to hand her back the eye patch. "I guess this one's lucky."

"Well, I'll be a gargoyle's grandma."

Martha took the patch with a shaky smile and tears of joy. Then she wiped her eyes and shoved the patch back into her hair. She was still so confused and didn't understand how a simple hand-sewn eyepatch *(that she had sewn)* could protect anyone from an arrow, especially someone as small as Lucas. But there was nothing simple about that eye patch. Martha had been wearing *that one* for so long, and practicing all sorts of magic while doing so, that it must have absorbed some of that magic, and that's what had protected Lucas— dumb luck and Grandma's clumsy magic.

"Oh, sweet, clever boy!" she shouted with laughter, grabbing his cheeks and showering him with kisses.

"OK, OK, Grandma," Lucas said with a laugh.

But Martha couldn't stop showering him with affection. She didn't want to. She was so happy her grandson was alive and unharmed. As he wiggled away from her kisses, Lucas noticed Bubbles standing there with a smoldering look, as if she was posing for a photo shoot.

Lucas pointed, wondering who she was.

Bubbles was waiting for Martha to give her another grand introduction as she had done for Jamie—but now wasn't the time for grand introductions.

"There's a lot I need to explain to you," Martha said. "And I will—later. But right now, your mom needs our help."

"What do you mean?" he asked. "What are you talking about, Grandma?"

129

Lucas looked for his mom but didn't see her. All he saw was her melted towel lying in the dirt. He looked up at his grandmother.

"Where is she?" he asked, worried. "Where's Mom?"

Martha took a deep breath and helped Lucas to his feet. Once standing, Lucas looked around at all the destruction surrounding the area. Even though the forest was calm again, the damage had already been done. And if these woods weren't creepy enough, now, *they were terrifying*. There was a burning stench that filled the air. Whole trees were knocked down, roots and all; some had even shattered into splinters. And there were claw marks longer than him everywhere, scratched deep into the dirt. *What could've done something like this?* he thought. He couldn't believe what he was seeing.

"Mahahahaha," Bubbles bleated, which meant, "We need to go!"

"*Mahahahaha*," Martha bleated back, which meant, "Hang on! Don't get your udders in a twist."

Lucas looked at his grandmother with questions and pointed at Bubbles a second time.

"As I said," Martha repeated, "there's a lot to explain."

But Trinity didn't think so. She felt she could sum it up quickly and that it should be addressed before they went any further. She thought Lucas needed to know the truth. She was positive he would have a meltdown after hearing everything she was about to say and that it was better to just get it over with now.

"Move it, witch," she said jokingly as she nudged her grandmother out of the way. "I got this." She then quickly caught Lucas up to speed, beginning with Bubbles. She pointed. "Don't ask me how, but that's Grandma's goat, Bubbles. She saved us."

Bubbles, acting like a hotshot, waved with a boastful look. Lucas waved back.

"Grandma brought us to this creepy forest," Trinity continued. "She has a witch's broom that apparently teleports people."

Martha raised her broom, and Lucas's eyes widened.

"I know, right?" Trinity said. "Also, Mom thought you were dead and got really mad, like *super mad*, went totally deranged, turned into a *freakin' dragon*, and ate that big butt sniffer on a horse. You know—that big scary dude in black armor who thought my phone was 'sorcery.' Now we have to help Grandma stop her before she eats more people and figure out how to change her back. Oh, and she breathes fire too."

"Mahahahaha," Bubbles bleated, adding one more thing.

"Yes," Martha agreed. "And we need to figure out a way home."

Whoa! Lucas thought. *What an earful.* After hearing everything his sister said, though, he reacted much differently than she'd thought he would.

"Well, what are we waiting for?" Lucas asked without hesitation, ready to do whatever was needed to save his mom. He was quite chipper about it too.

"Mahahahaha!" Bubbles bleated loudly, which meant, "Attaboy!" She liked his can-do attitude and warrior spirit.

"Mahahahaha," she bleated again. This time, telling Martha to use her broom so they could travel as fast as possible.

Martha agreed. It *would* be much faster. "But I can't," she said. "Even if I wanted to. The broom is useless to us for now. For my broom to work, I can only travel to a place I've already been or at least a place I can see."

Since Martha had never been to the castle and there was no way for her to see over the hill, especially from within the forest, her broom wasn't an option. But they were in luck. There was someone with them who *had* been to the castle.

"I think I can help," Gretchen intervened. "My sister and I have stood before the castle doors many times, wondering what living on the other side might be like. Perhaps that is close enough to make your special broom work?"

"That's brilliant!" Martha shouted with a smile. "Just brilliant!"

There was no time to waste. Martha told everyone to grab the broom and hold on tight. But before they could do so, Martha stopped them. She wasn't ready to travel just yet. There was still one thing left to do.

"Hang on," she said. "We're going to need some extra help."

"Extra help?" Lucas repeated. "Who's going to help *us*?"

"Well, I know one person." Martha sighed, not knowing if that person would be *willing* to help.

"Who?" he asked.

"It's better if I show you."

Martha tilted her head back; took a deep, deep breath; flared her nostrils wide; and summoned Sparkly Martha once more.

Boogers and snot flew everywhere as Martha blew her nose wildly into the air! Gretchen and Philine looked at each other and shrugged. But, again, they weren't going to try to understand what was going on. Lucas and Bubbles laughed, though it was disgusting. Even Peanut Butter peeked out of Martha's hair and chuckled a squeaky chuckle. But Trinity didn't think it was funny.

"Ugh, Grandma!" She grunted loudly with a sour face. "What was the point of that?"

But before Martha could answer, Trinity felt a tap on her shoulder and turned around. There before her stood Sparkly Martha, in all her sparkly wonder. Lucas's eyes lit up with bewilderment. Trinity remained cool, pretending she wasn't impressed.

"Mahahahaha," Bubbles bleated, which meant, "Good to see you again, Sparkles."

Sparkly Martha nodded back.

Since Sparkly Martha was made with Martha's magic, *she* also understood goat and recognized Bubbles immediately in her human form.

Gretchen and Philine waved nervously with a smile, and Sparkly Martha waved back. Lucas reached out to touch the colorful glowing sparkles, but Trinity quickly slapped his hand.

"Ouch!" Lucas said, rubbing his hand. "Why'd you do that?"

"Because," Trinity said. "You can't just grab her sparkles like that! Women have rights." She looked at Sparkly Martha, unsure how to explain what kind of a woman she was. "Even a sparkly woman who's made of magic and flies out of an old lady's nose, you need to ask before you touch." But Trinity didn't feel the same way when it came to capturing images, whether it was intrusive or without permission. She pulled out her phone and snapped a quick photo.

"I'm sorry," he said. He reached his hand out toward Sparkly Martha but asked permission this time. "Can I touch your sparkles, please, colorful sand lady?"

Sparkly Martha nodded yes.

Lucas's fingers passed through Sparkly Martha's sparkles like passing through a small ocean of tiny twinkles. Her sparkles tickled his skin as each sparkly speck danced around his hand. It felt like a thousand little butterflies kissing him all at once.

"Allow me to introduce you all," Martha said. "This is my magical helper, Sparkly Martha. Sparkly Martha, these are my grandchildren, Lucas and Trinity, and these two are our new friends, Gretchen and Philine."

Lucas and Trinity shared a confused look. "What do you mean, *magical helper*?" Trinity asked."

"Well, you know," Martha replied. "She's like—my assistant, but magical. Helps me with the day-by-day tasks. Assists me in conjuring spells. Gives me a hand mixing the occasional potion. Keeps a checklist of the items in my hair." She put her hand in front of her mouth, so Sparkly Martha couldn't read her lips and mumbled, "And she does a little cleaning here and there."

Trinity and Lucas looked at each other. They knew what an assistant was, but they still had so many questions—like why *her* assistant lived in her nose.

"How is *this* going to help us?" Trinity asked, pointing at Sparkly Martha. "This is just glitter from your nose?" She looked at Sparkly Martha. "No offense."

Sparkly Martha nodded as if to say, "None taken." She had been called much worse by Martha.

But Martha didn't feel like she was explaining it well enough to her grandchildren and thought they'd understand better if she compared her helper to something a little more familiar. She hated stereotypes, but a black cat was the best comparison she could come up with.

"You know how *everybody* thinks witches have a black cat?" she asked, rolling her eyes.

"OK?" both her grandchildren responded.

"Well, she's like my black cat, and let's leave it at that. Trust me. She can help."

Gretchen and Philine were as confused as Lucas and Trinity but didn't ask questions.

Sparkly Martha gestured with a nod, stating it was a pleasure to meet everyone, even though she, too, didn't like being compared to a flea-ridden feline.

Peanut Butter popped out of Martha's hair for a quick second, and murmured, "Herro," with a squeak before hiding again.

Martha then explained the situation to Sparkly Martha, summing it up quickly, the same way Trinity had done for Lucas. She told her how Jamie had turned into a dragon and gone on a rampage of destruction after she thought the Duke had killed Lucas. "It's up to us to help her," she said, begging for Sparkly Martha's help. "We need to show Jamie that Lucas is *alive* and try to change her back before it's too late. Many lives are at stake."

After feeling the presence of dark magic and seeing the destruction all around her, Sparkly Martha knew how serious Martha's plea for help truly was. And although the situation wasn't ideal, she was secretly excited to finally be able to use her magical talents—on something other than boring household chores. She was in!

So, with Sparkly Martha on board, Martha was now ready to travel. She held out her broom and told everyone to grab hold. She then told Gretchen to focus and think really hard about the castle. "Hocus Pocus, *focus, focus, focus.*"

And that's exactly what Gretchen did. She closed her eyes, holding the broom with one hand and her sister close with the other, and thought hard about the castle doors. Once Martha was confident Gretchen had a good image in her head, she quickly plucked a single bristle, and—*poof!*—they all disappeared in a red puff of smoke.

CHAPTER FIFTEEN

AT THE CASTLE

Poof! In an orange puff of smoke, Martha and the others reappeared in front of the castle, right before the very doors Gretchen was thinking about, and just in the nick of time. The dragon hadn't arrived yet, but it was close. Martha could feel its presence.

Lucas and Trinity were in awe as they looked up. Neither of them had ever seen a real castle before, and this one was so magnificent and *so big*.

"This must've taken a hundred years to build," Lucas said to Trinity, who agreed with a nod, never once taking her eyes off the castle.

Each stone was bigger than both of them, at least twice in size, and it seemed like there were millions, stacked on top of millions, stacked on top of millions more. The only two things not made of stone were the incredibly large swinging doors that arched together to form what looked like one *colossal* door, wider than the widest elephant and taller than the tallest giraffe.

"I bet only a giant can open those doors," Lucas said excitedly.

"Not a giant," Gretchen chimed in. "But it does take the strength of twenty men."

"Wow," he said.

Trinity pulled out her phone and snapped a quick photo.

"No time to daydream!" Martha told her grandchildren, who were gobsmacked by this wondrous sight. "We have work to do!"

She shoved her wonky broom deep into her hair and dug around her curls for a bit. When she was done digging, she pulled out a small, clear glass vial no bigger than her palm filled with a potion that looked like liquid silver. She quickly popped out the cork plugging the vial, threw her head back, and ...

Bottoms up!

She drank the potion like a hot shot of soapy water. "Blah!" she moaned with a shiver from the stomach-turning taste. "Yuck!" She then put the vial back into her hair so she could reuse it at a later time (clear glass vials were a high-demand item that didn't come cheap and were often very hard to find at the witches' market). After swallowing every bit of the unsavory potion, her stomach rumbled—and a moment later—she belched a small gray cloud the size of a softball that remained floating in place. *Burrrp!*

"Ooh, excuse me," Martha said, clearing her throat and patting her chest.

"Awesome, Grandma." Lucas giggled.

"You know it," she replied, licking her lips as if the burp was tasty. But it definitely was not!

"Is that an actual burp cloud?" Trinity asked, unimpressed and very grossed out. "First the booger lady, and now this? How's a nasty burp cloud supposed to help us anyway?"

Martha didn't reply. She looked at Trinity from the corner of her eye and smirked her granny lips—because this wasn't some *ordinary*, disgusting burp cloud—this was a *magical*, disgusting burp cloud. Big difference! She grabbed the floating cloud with puckered lips and slurped it up like spaghetti, and as she did, all the blue in her eyes faded away before turning gray, and her entire body swelled like a hot air balloon. The more and more she slurped up the cloud, the bigger she became. *Sllrrrp. Sllrrrp. Sllrrrp.* Bigger. Bigger. Bigger. She grew bigger and rounder than humanly possible, like a giant inflatable ball—and she continued to grow!

When it seemed like Martha's body had stretched to its limit and was about to pop, she released the cloud as a powerful fog— blowing it out of her mouth like a stormy gust of wind billowing into the air.

She blew and blew and blew—until she deflated herself from the giant balloon shape she'd become and was as skinny as a pencil and as flat as paper and could blow no more.

Lucas and Trinity looked up, amazed and humored. "Whoa!" they said together.

"That was so cool!" Lucas said.

"Never doubted you for a second," Trinity said with confidence.

"Yeah—*sure*," Martha replied sarcastically to Trinity, and with her thumb in her mouth, puffed herself back to normal size.

Now, the entire castle and its surroundings were hidden behind a thick blanket of fog. Of course, this wouldn't stop the ferocious dragon from its path of destruction, but it would help keep the people of the kingdom safe—at least for a short while.

"This will buy us some time," Martha said. "But we still need to get inside the castle and warn whoever's in charge. There must be a king inside."

"Uh, or a queen," Trinity pointed out.

"Yes," Martha agreed, correcting herself. "King *or* queen."

"Thank you," Trinity said. "Now, how are you planning on getting in there?"

"Yeah," Lucas said, wondering the same thing. "How? There's no way we can open those doors. They're enormous!"

Martha was going to suggest that Bubbles use her strength to open the doors, but before she had the chance to do so …

Sparkly Martha took matters into her own sparkly hands, nodding as if to say, "I'm on it!" and quickly sprang into action.

Oh boy, Martha thought, immediately expecting things to go wrong.

In a dash, Sparkly Martha swirled over to Bubbles and wrapped herself around her as tightly as she could, magically shifting into a great big set of sparkly wings. Bubbles had no idea what Sparkly Martha was up to but went along without flinching. Sparkly Martha then flapped and flapped and *flapped, flapped, flapped* those wings with all her might, lifting Bubbles from the ground, *up, up, up*, until they were high in the air—then the two of them made their way over the castle with ease. Martha and the others watched as they flew out of sight.

"Well," Martha said. "That's one way, I guess."

"What now, Grandma?" Lucas asked.

"I dunno," she said, looking up at the castle. "I guess we just wait."

But they wouldn't have to wait for long. Soon, the great big doors to the castle opened wide, loudly creaking and squeaking as they opened.

"Wow, she actually did it?" Martha said, surprised. She looked at Lucas and smiled. "That was quick. I'm impressed!"

Martha had been wrong to doubt Sparkly Martha. She was indeed impressed, especially with how swiftly Sparkly Martha and Bubbles had acted—until the castle doors were fully open—and it was revealed that Sparkly Martha and Bubbles had done something very naughty.

They had taken the king hostage!

As they came out of the castle, Bubbles was carrying the young king by the back of his collar, against his will, like a helpless puppy. She was even wearing his little gold crown and smiling proudly.

Trinity thought it was quite hysterical. She pulled out her phone, laughing, and snapped a quick photo.

Martha, on the other hand, didn't find it amusing one bit. She was no longer impressed, nor was she smiling.

She was outraged.

"Are you kidding me?" she shouted angrily. "Cinnamon sticks! Cinnamon sticks! Cinnamon sticks!"

Sparkly Martha and Bubbles looked at each other, confused. They didn't understand why Martha was so upset *or* why she was using such profanity.

"Mahahahaha," Bubbles bleated, which meant, "You wanted the king. *Well*—here he is."

But that wasn't what Martha wanted at all.

"I wanted to *warn* the king!" she shouted. *"Warn him!* I didn't want you to *kidnap* him. He's just a child! What were you thinking?"

Bubbles and Sparkly Martha looked at each other, still confused, and then both looked at Martha. There was no way either one of them could have warned the king, even if they'd wanted to.

"Mahahahaha," Bubbles bleated, which meant, "You're the only one here who speaks goat."

And Sparkly Martha nodded, adding that she only uses body language.

"Good point," Martha answered after a brief pause, realizing she hadn't thought that through. "OK, my bad. But put him down, please."

Bubbles immediately released the king and humbly handed him his crown back. Martha felt terrible and tried to explain herself to the king. But before she could …

Swarms of people came running toward the castle in a panic, screaming in terror as Martha's burp fog began to fade.

The king didn't need an explanation. He saw with his own eyes a glimpse of what the people in his kingdom were running from. He saw the fierce, bloodthirsty dragon in the sky, breathing fire that scorched the earth it flew over.

The king's soldiers were also returning, even the Duke's horse and the villagers. Without the Duke to stop them, the soldiers had helped the villagers escape. Each soldier carried as many people as possible on their horse and rode like the wind. But the dragon was right on top of them. So whatever Martha was going to do, she needed to do it now!

"OK, my friend," Martha said as she pulled Peanut Butter from her hair. "Ride's over."

She handed Peanut Butter over to the king, who instantly became smitten with the furry creature.

"Herro," Peanut Butter murmured.

"This is Peanut Butter," Martha said to the king. "Keep this creature safe, your majesty."

"I will," the king assured her.

Gretchen and Philine offered to stay with the king and help in any way they could, to which the king agreed. Martha told Trinity she should do the same thing, *but no way was that happening.*

"I don't think so!" Trinity said. "After everything we've been through this morning, I'm seeing this all the way through. I already lost my brother once. I won't lose him again."

Martha knew there was no point in arguing. She could tell that Trinity had made up her mind, and she knew better than to try to reason with a stubborn teenager.

"OK, then," Martha said. She placed her hands on Lucas's shoulders. "Let's go show your mom you're alive—*and hope that works.*"

"Wait, what was that last part?" Lucas asked with worry.

"Nothing," Martha replied casually and then pounded her chest like a gorilla. "Let's do this!" She looked at Bubbles and Sparkly Martha, who were standing off to the side, unsure of what to do. "Well, are you two coming?"

Sparkly Martha and Bubbles looked at each other. They perked up with a smile and readied themselves for battle as they joined Martha and her grandchildren. While everyone else ran toward the castle for safety, the five of them, together, walked away from it, out into the open, toward the danger, ready to save Jamie from the dragon she'd become—or die trying.

CHAPTER SIXTEEN

BADGE OF COURAGE

Martha didn't waste any time trying to get the dragon's attention. Once they were out in the open and away from the castle, she pulled back her sleeves, ready to conjure some magic, and went straight to work. She removed both of her gloves, yanking them with her fingertips and jamming them into her hair for safekeeping. She then slid her patch to the other eye and put on her game face.

"Here goes nothing," she said, taking a deep breath. She threw her hands in the air as if she was trying to reach a bottled spell on the top shelf and wiggled, wiggled, *wiggled* her fingers.

"Flaming hot magic, I call on you. Come to Granny—a blazing blue!"

She hocked up a goopy loogie and spat it directly into her hands.

"*Ugh*," Trinity said in disgust, who thought this was nastier than the burp cloud, *way* nastier.

But Martha was too busy concentrating to pay her any mind. Besides, this loogie was important—a way to grease the wheels. She continued to conjure, clapping her hands and pressing them together as tightly as possible, trying to create the best friction. Then she rubbed her hands together like two campfire sticks, *really, really fast*, to heat them up—and they soon became red hot with smoke. She blew into her hands and continued rubbing them together, faster and faster. She never stopped once. *Rub rub rub rub rub rub ...*

She rubbed and rubbed and rubbed until—*whoosh!*—her hands suddenly burst into bright, dazzling blue flames.

"Holy cow!" Lucas shouted. "Your hands are on fire! *Blue fire!*"

Trinity was speechless.

Both her grandchildren worried the flames might burn, but Martha assured them there was nothing to worry about. The flames were magical and not painful. Not one bit. And since there was nothing to be concerned about, Trinity pulled out her phone and snapped a photo.

"I'm definitely posting this if we ever make it back home," she said. "Hashtag *HOT GRANDMA*."

Lucas laughed.

Martha looked up to the sky. All the fog was now completely gone. "Hey, Lucas," she said with a grin. "Check this out!"

She waited for the dragon to show itself. And as soon as it did, she reared her shoulder back and, with all her might, really putting her back into it, *flung her arm straight up.*

"Hadouken!" She lit up the sky like the Fourth of July as she hurled a great big fireball into the air. Then another. And another! And another after that!

Lucas laughed and laughed, dancing next to his grandmother while copying her moves. But then he stopped after realizing what she was doing—*and who she was doing it to.*

"Will that hurt Mom?" he asked.

"Not a chance," Martha assured him, throwing fireball after fireball. *"Hadouken! Hadouken!* Besides, I'm not trying to hit her.

I'm only trying to get her attention. *Hadouken!* So that she heads toward us instead of the castle. *Hadouken! Hadouken! Hadouken! Hadouken! Hadouken!* Once she sees you're alive, I'm certain she will calm down and return to normal." Martha crossed her fiery fingers superstitiously. "Or so I hope," she whispered to herself.

"Mahahahaha," Bubbles bleated to Martha, which meant, "What about us? What do you want us to do?"

"Stay with my grandchildren!" Martha shouted. "Keep them safe! Sparkly Martha, you can help me with the dragon."

Sparkly Martha nodded and swooped into action, flying swiftly into the sky, half-cocked, without a plan once again. She flew head-on, directly toward the dragon, shifting into thousands of little sparkling bees. Her little bee wings buzzed boldly all the way up—and as soon as she met the threat in the sky—she bravely swarmed around the dragon's fearsome face, buzzing and stinging its eyes, using every single stinger she had. *Buzz! Buzz! Sting! Sting! Buzz! Buzz! Sting! Sting!* It was the only part of the dragon's body not protected by scales.

This foolish effort only agitated the dragon. It scratched and clawed at Sparkly Martha, trying to extinguish her with its fiery breath while flapping its mighty wings through the air. As it did, fireballs from below exploded one after the other.

Kaboom! Kaboom! Kaboom!

With all this fire coming at her from every direction, it was too hot for Sparkly Martha to stick around. So she quickly shifted again—this time to her usual sparkly self—and swooped back down to the ground, far away from the heat, while still trying to lure the dragon. But the dragon didn't follow.

Martha continued, relentlessly throwing her magical fire into the sky. She flung fireball after fireball after fireball, desperately trying to draw the dragon's attention. If *Sparkly Martha* couldn't annoy the dragon into following her, then Martha didn't have a clue as to what else would work. But she kept on, fireball after fireball after fireball. Soon, however, she became tired, and her magic grew weak. Her arms now felt like long wet noodles and were completely useless. She had no strength left in them whatsoever. But she *still* didn't quit. She managed to throw one final fireball before her flaming hands fizzled out. And though her fire had fizzled, Martha was able to draw the dragon's attention with that final fireball.

Having noticed her, the dragon had now set its sights on Martha, hurling toward her with great speed, roaring and furiously breathing fire the entire way down.

"OK," Martha said nervously, hoping for the best outcome. "Here we go!" She winked at Bubbles, *a witch's wink*, hinting she was about to do something foolish.

Without warning, Martha grabbed Lucas, and with Bubbles's help, the two lifted him high, making sure the dragon had a clear visual.

"Wait! Wait! What are you doing?" he shouted.

"Showing your mom you're still alive," Martha answered.

"Not like this! Put me down! Put me down!"

But Martha didn't put him down. "If you have a better idea, I'm all ears," she said. "If not, this is happening."

"I don't!" he shouted, squirming like a worm on a hook.

"OK," Martha said. "Then here goes nothing." She cocked her head with her mouth to the side and whispered into her hair.

"Listen up. Please don't say no. Granny needs you one last time—to grow, grow, grow!"

And just like that—her hair suddenly came to life and stretched out before her once again, each curl binding together, twisting and twirling and tightening, strand by strand, as it stretched, and finally—shaped itself into a giant, hairy, *megaphone*. Trinity used her skills as a cheerleader to lend a hand by lifting the hairy megaphone and resting it on her shoulders, but not before pulling out her phone and snapping a quick photo. With her hairy megaphone and Trinity's help, Martha was able to magically amplify her voice, loud enough to reach and penetrate the dragon's eardrums. She took a deep breath, puckered her lips properly to get the best vocal range, pressed them against her hair, and spoke.

"Jamie! Jamie, look! It's Lucas! He's not dead! He's alive! You must change back!"

But nothing happened. There wasn't a single change. Jamie was still a fire-breathing dragon—*and still heading straight toward them at full speed.*

151

"Uh-oh," Martha said.

"Uh-oh?" Lucas repeated, still lifted in the air.

"What do you mean, uh-oh?" Trinity asked. "I thought you said this would work!"

"I thought it would," Martha replied as her hair slithered back to normal.

But then Martha had another idea, *worse* than the one before. "I know!" She looked over at Bubbles. "Let's wiggle him!" she said.

"Mahahahaha?" Bubbles bleated, which meant, "What do you mean, wiggle him?"

"You know," Martha said, giving a demonstration by shaking her hips. "Wiggle him."

Bubbles shrugged her shoulders and bleated, "Mahahahaha," which meant, "OK."

The two began wiggling Lucas like fish bait. But this was no fish they were trying to catch. Still, they wiggled him. *Wiggle! Wiggle! Wiggle!* He held on to his glasses as his eyeballs rattled up and down and side to side from all the wiggling. It was too much to handle! They wiggled him and wiggled him and wiggled him until he couldn't stand to be wiggled anymore. But it still wasn't working, and the dragon was near. All hope seemed to be lost.

Then—Lucas had an idea of his own.

"Put me down, Grandma!" he shouted. "I know what to do."

But there was no more time. If they didn't get into the castle quickly, all of them would soon become dragon food for sure. So Martha and Bubbles put Lucas down, and Martha reached into her hair and pulled out her wonky broom.

"There's no time!" Martha shouted, gripping the broom tightly. "I'm sorry! But we must go *now*."

They were seconds away from being eaten.

"No, Grandma!" Lucas insisted, still wobbly from the wiggling as he tried to regain his balance. "I want my mom back!" He grabbed Martha by the hand. "Trust me, Grandma. I know what to do. I have a secret weapon up my sleeve."

Martha looked at her broom—then at Lucas—trying to decide the best action to take. But in her heart, she already knew what to do. She stuffed the broom back into her hair, and on a great leap of faith, she placed all of her hope and trust in her grandson. "I trust you, sweetheart," she said to him with a smile.

"Me too," Trinity added with a wink.

"Mahahahaha," Bubbles bleated, which meant, "You got this, kid."

Sparkly Martha nodded her approval as well.

Lucas was nervous but confident, knowing he had their trust. He pushed his glasses to his face and took a deep breath. Then he turned and took a few steps forward on shaky legs and looked up. The dragon was upon him, its murderous mouth wide open, hissing and growling savagely. Smoke and flames erupted as it readied to gobble Lucas up. Trinity hid her frightened eyes against her grandmother. "I can't watch!" she cried.

Lucas didn't have anything up his sleeve like he had mentioned to his grandmother, not literally. But he did have a secret weapon— guarded inside his front right pocket. He had been carrying it with him this entire time. It was his dad's old police badge, Lucas's prized possession. He reached into his pocket, clutched the badge in hand, took a deep breath, and slowly pulled it out, hoping it would help remind his mom of the family she still had and who she was

inside—and change her
back. He looked at the shiny silver badge, raising it close to
his face—but didn't see his reflection looking back
at him. Instead—he saw his dad—and
it gave him courage.

"I could really use your help,"
Lucas said with a sad smile.

A single teardrop rolled down Lucas's
cheek as the dragon closed in. He wiped
it away, puffed his chest out valiantly,
and held the badge as high as he could,
immediately feeling ten times bigger and ten
times stronger—as if the badge was a shield
that could protect him from any harm. He truly
expected this gesture of hope, this memory of his dad, to
somehow be enough. But still—nothing happened. The dragon
didn't even notice the tiny piece of tin Lucas was holding. And now,
with all hope lost—it was over.

He turned his head away and squeezed his eyes shut, dropping to the ground and curling into a ball—but he kept his dad's badge in hand, gripped tightly, and held high.

Luckily, a bright ray of sunlight miraculously reflected off the badge in the nick of time and beamed directly into the dragon's eye, blinding it and throwing it off course.

It roared in anger while trying to turn its long neck away from the bright light, but Lucas stayed vigilant with his hand in the air. This mere inconvenience still didn't stop the beast, though. The bright light was no match for this monster's insatiable appetite for death. Martha knew she had to help. But how? Her magic had fizzled out with the fireballs. Perhaps *she* also had one last trick of her own up *her* sleeve. Whatever she was going to do, she needed to act fast. So, *in a lickety-split of a second*, she reached out her arm and pointed one finger toward Lucas, focusing her aim on the badge— *and blasted the last bit of magic she could muster, racing forward like a speeding bullet*—hoping it was enough.

And it was!

With Martha's final blast of magic, she was able to magnify the reflecting light, making it shine brighter than a thousand and one suns (without the harmful radiation or heat). The intensely bright light was too much for the dragon, impairing every one of its senses completely. It twisted and turned its body in agony, trying to move in all directions, unable to escape.

This was it! The dragon had been bested.

It plummeted—like a mosquito after an encounter with a porch zapper. It fell hard and heavy, crashing into the ground like a meteor.

Before the dragon fell, Sparkly Martha was able to use her sparkles to form a dome-shaped shield over the group, protecting Martha and her family. And then it happened.

Boom! A giant mushroom cloud of dirt exploded as the dragon slammed down. The powerful impact sent shock waves throughout the kingdom. It could be seen for miles and miles! The earth quaked, the castle shook, and everyone felt it far and wide.

To say the least, it was a miracle that Sparkly Martha's sparkles held up against such a blast. But they did! Martha was very grateful to have such a good helper. Sparkly Martha then took it upon herself once she knew it was safe and jumped into action once more. She quickly shifted into a sparkly tornado, swirling about, and sucked away all the dirt clouding the air.

Martha and her family were unharmed, and surprisingly, Lucas was now standing on his own two feet, with his glasses still on his face. He opened his eyes and slowly turned his head, looking up, not knowing what to expect—and there she was, standing over him.

Jamie was her normal self once again, no longer a fierce, red, fire-breathing monster.

Lucas was triumphant!

The dragon had finally been defeated, and the dark magic Jamie carried inside surrendered back into hiding.

Lucas was so happy he didn't know what to say or how to react. He wiped his lenses and pushed his glasses to his face with a grin. "Hi, Mom," he said softly and handed her the badge.

CHAPTER SEVENTEEN

FAREWELL

Finally, it was over. The dragon was gone, and the kingdom was safe, all thanks to Lucas—well, with *a lot* of help from Grandma and her crew. But there was still one problem. Jamie was completely naked! Fortunately, that was a quick fix. Martha reached into her hair and pulled out a ridiculously oversized white T-shirt, big enough to cover a bear. She ran over to Jamie and quickly covered her. Coincidentally, the T-shirt read, "My mom's a witch."

"Really, Ma?" Jamie asked, looking down at the shirt, but she quickly laughed it off. Then, she looked at Lucas and dropped to her knees in tears. "I'm so sorry," she said, sobbing over him. "I thought I'd lost you. I don't know what happened. I ... I couldn't control myself."

"It's OK, Mom," Lucas said as his eyes also teared up. "It's not your fault. It's mine. When I ate Grandma's cake, I was thinking about the time Dad brought me to that medieval place I liked so much, and I just wanted him back. But I didn't mean for any of this to happen. I swear! It was an accident. I'm so sorry."

Jamie smiled and threw her arms around him, hugging his little body and squeezing him like there was no tomorrow. "It's not your fault. None of this is your fault. I miss him too."

As she continued to hug Lucas, she looked down and noticed the badge in her hand was completely covered in dirt. She looked closer, and *she, too,* saw her husband's reflection instead of her own. She immediately felt guilty for the condition it was in—remembering how he always kept it polished and shiny. So she wrapped the badge in her big, baggy shirt and polished it clean until all the dirt was entirely gone. There wasn't a single smudge or streak that could be seen. It was even shinier than before.

"Here," she said, handing it back to Lucas. "Good as new."

Trinity came running with her arms wide open and jumped on top of Lucas and her mom, knocking them both to the ground. Luckily, Lucas was able to place his dad's badge back inside his pocket before being knocked down, so it wouldn't get dirty again—*but of course,* he wasn't so lucky with his glasses. They flung off of his face once again. But he just laughed. They all did. Trinity picked them up and cleaned them before handing them over. He pushed them to his face and smiled. Jamie hugged both kids with a big smile herself, grateful to be with her family.

Martha stood off to the side, twiddling her thumbs and shuffling her feet while looking down.

Jamie looked up at her. "Well?" she said. *"Get in here."*

Martha smiled, kicking up the dirt with her feet as she joined them. They all hugged and rejoiced. It was the perfect ending to a terrible, terrible morning. They held each other for a while longer, and then slowly, they all stood.

Bubbles and Sparkly Martha walked over, and Martha introduced them to Jamie, though she had *already* introduced Bubbles earlier that morning in her goat form.

"Jamie," Martha said. "This is my helper, Sparkly Martha, and I believe you've met Bubbles." There was a brief *but awkward* silence as the three stared at each other.

Then Jamie broke that silence. "I feel like I already know you both so well," she said. "I don't know how to explain it."

Sparkly Martha happily nodded as if she felt the same way. Bubbles, however, had a look on her face like she was still cross with Jamie. After all, Jamie had said some not-so-nice things about her earlier that morning. But to Bubbles's surprise, Jamie quickly made amends.

Jamie looked at Bubbles. "I have to apologize," she said, "for all the mean and hurtful things I said earlier this morning. I didn't mean any of it. I was just angry and sad, and I took my feelings out on you. But there's no excuse for how I behaved. I know what you did here today to help my mom and my children, and I can't thank you enough. Friends?" She reached out, offering her hand.

"Mahahahaha," Bubbles bleated, which meant, "Friends." She humorously slapped Jamie's hand away like a brute and gave her a big, *big* hug instead, with the strength of fifty goats, squeezing and lifting her off the ground.

Now they were square. After all, she *had* peed on Jamie. And though Jamie's words were cruel and insensitive, and uncalled for, they weren't nearly as bad as goat pee.

Once they were certain the danger was gone, Gretchen and Philine came out of the castle with the king, who was still holding Peanut Butter, keeping him safe as he'd promised. While Gretchen was with him, she explained what had been happening outside the castle and far beyond the stretches of his kingdom. She told him about all the terrible things the Duke had done and all the people who'd suffered at his hands, including her and her sister.

After hearing the horror stories about the Duke, the king vowed to offer help and protection to anyone within his kingdom who needed or wanted it and promised to keep the doors to the castle open for good. As a further show of his great kindness, Gretchen and Philine were invited to live in the castle and act as personal advisors to the king. Together, they could help him grow his kingdom into a prosperous and peaceful place for all.

"You are all welcome here anytime you wish," the king told Martha and the others.

"Thank you," Martha said. She looked over at Lucas with a smile. "But we won't be making *wishes* anytime soon."

Martha and Lucas laughed. But the King had a troubled look, and Martha noticed it.

"What is it?" Martha asked.

"Well," the king said. "I don't know how to explain to my people what happened here today. I myself do not fully understand what I saw."

All of the soldiers and villagers hiding in the castle began to walk out one by one. They, too, looked confused, walking around like clueless zombies. The king glanced at them and then looked at Martha with a heavy heart. He may have been a king, but he was still only a kid.

"I don't know what to do." He sighed, looking down.

"Don't worry," Martha said, assuring him everything would be fine. "You don't have to do a thing."

"I *don't?*" he asked, confused and curious as to why not.

"Nope," she replied, lifting her eyepatch with a wink. She then slid it to the other eye and lowered it back down. "They're all going to forget very shortly."

The king and Lucas giggled at her sliding the eye patch.

"What of us?" Gretchen asked. "Will we forget as well?"

"Do you want to forget?" Martha asked.

Gretchen and Philine looked at each other and then looked at the king.

"We would like to remember if that is OK?" Gretchen said.

Philine nodded, agreeing with her sister.

The king wanted to remember as well. "So would I," he said, rubbing Peanut Butter's fluffy fur. "I don't want to forget my new friend." He lifted and held Peanut Butter against his chest.

"OK then," Martha said. "It's settled. You, your sister, and you, Your Highness, will remember everything that happened here today. *Everyone else* will forget."

"What about Peanut Butter?" the king asked with concern.

"Don't worry," she assured him, hunched over, tickling Peanut Butter's belly and quickly pinching the king's cheeks—the way grandmothers do. "I sense this one's impervious to magic and will forget nothing."

The king still looked nervous. So, Martha decided to give him a little something to remind him that he was, after all, a kid. And hopefully, this small token of hers would help him find that kid inside himself. It wasn't much, but she had a witch's sense he might enjoy it. She reached into her hair and pulled out a small, magical, never-ending jar of Texas-made creamy peanut butter and happily tossed it to the king. That way, he could enjoy mouthful after mouthful for as long as he liked.

"A yummy parting gift," she said. "Soon, everything will be back to normal."

The king looked at the jar of peanut butter. It was unlike anything he'd ever seen before.

"You don't know what you're missing," Trinity told the king. "That's good stuff. Unless you have a nut allergy."

The king looked baffled. *"A nut allergy?"*

Trinity smirked. "You'll find out soon enough if you have one."

Then, Martha gave Sparkly Martha *a piercing look*, one like never before. And with that look, Sparkly Martha was completely compliant for the first time ever. Though she knew she wouldn't like doing what it was Martha wanted her to do, she didn't argue one bit. She didn't mutter a single sparkle. She did Martha's bidding at once and promptly flew through the air, scattering her sparkles over the entire land. She was everywhere, instantly, and would soon be in everyone's nose! It was her worst nightmare come to life. But it had to be done. So she revved up her sparkles—as sparkly as sparkling possible—until she had all the people's attention. Then she got down to business! Once everybody was looking up, mesmerized by the flickering wonder she'd cast over them, she infiltrated their noses—hundreds of noses all at once—and in a swift, heroic plunge—*she was gone.* Every single person, far and wide, began sniffling with the itches—and sneezed at exactly the same time.

Achoo!

And just like that—they all forgot. Not a single person in the kingdom, not even the villagers outside the kingdom, remembered a dragon, magic, or anything about the strangers who fell from the sky. It was as though it had never happened.

All that was left for them to do now was make a hasty getaway.

"We need to go before someone sees us," Martha said. "If we stick around, people may begin to remember, and I think it'll be a long while before my helper ever goes up another nose."

So they set off.

The king, Gretchen, and Philine waved goodbye as they said their final farewells. Peanut Butter waved its furry little paw goodbye as well. Lucas and Trinity were sad to leave but knew they had to.

Martha reached into her hair and pulled out her wonky broom. Bubbles, Jamie, Lucas, and Trinity each grabbed hold. Martha closed her eyes and thought of home. She then plucked a single bristle, and—*poof!*—they all disappeared in a pink puff of smoke.

CHAPTER EIGHTEEN

HOME

Poof! Seconds later, Martha and the others reappeared in a white puff of smoke back inside Martha's house, and were now standing in the middle of her living room, or what was left of it.

Jamie was able to hold her stomach this time, but she still didn't like Martha's way of traveling one bit. "Phew," she said, relieved it was finally over. "I hope I never have to do that again." But then she looked around, a bit thrown off by what she saw. She thought everything would magically fix itself and go back to normal now that she was no longer a dragon. But things were nowhere near normal. Martha's house was still in shambles.

Not even Bubbles had changed. She was still in human form.

Lucas and Trinity walked over to the window and looked outside. Not only had everything *not* magically poofed back to normal, but the timeline hadn't changed either. They were still in the small, isolated village where they'd landed that morning.

"We're still back in the olden days," Lucas said with a shrug.

"What gives, Grandma?" Trinity asked.

Martha didn't answer. She was well aware of where they were. She simply attempted to smile while looking down at all of her things, broken and scattered on the floor. Her demeanor had drastically changed. She became sad-looking and lost. She handed her broom to Bubbles and then slowly walked around her living room, sorting through the mess as she scooted her furniture back to how it was before, or so she tried, never saying a word.

Jamie looked at her kids, confused by her mom's behavior. "What's going on with your grandmother?" she whispered.

Lucas and Trinity shrugged. "Dunno," they said. They were just as confused.

Jamie looked over at Bubbles, who also shrugged and bleated, "Mahahahah," which meant, "I've never seen her like this. Don't ask me."

But Jamie didn't understand her because she didn't speak goat. So she went straight to the source. "What's going on with you, Ma?" she asked, concerned.

"Oh, nothing." Martha sighed. Something was definitely wrong. She continued trying to unclutter the mess, but her thoughts were clearly elsewhere.

"Ma?" Jamie said, speaking louder this time, trying not to sound too pushy, especially after all the trouble she had caused. "I thought you were going to get us home with your broom?"

Martha stopped what she was doing and looked at her broom, which Bubbles was still holding. "And I will," she assured Jamie. But she wasn't even sure she had the power to do so—and getting her family back home wasn't the only thing on her mind.

"Then why are we still here?" Jamie asked.

Martha abruptly walked out of the room without answering and went down the hall.

On the floor in the hallway was the framed photo from the wall of a boy in a pond holding a fish. The frame was broken, and the glass was shattered, so Martha pulled the photo out and dusted it with a bundle of her curls. Moments later, she returned to the living room, holding the photo to her chest, and *then* answered Jamie.

"The truth is, this house *is* my home," she said. "We're still here … because … I couldn't leave it behind. Or this photo. It's the only one I have, and I refuse to take away its authenticity by using magic to duplicate it. So when I thought of home, this is where my broom brought us all—*my home*."

"That's not true, Ma," Jamie said. She looked at her kids— then back at her mom. She took a deep breath. *"We're* your home."

Martha was moved by her daughter's sentiment. And though her timing may have been off, as it usually was, she felt that

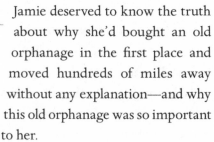

Jamie deserved to know the truth about why she'd bought an old orphanage in the first place and moved hundreds of miles away without any explanation—and why this old orphanage was so important to her.

She handed Jamie the photo and delivered some very unexpected news. "This is where I met your father," she said. With watery eyes, she looked down at the old macaroni necklace around her neck and twiddled the string between her fingers. She smiled as her tears trickled down her face.

She looked around the room, recalling old memories, such as her first day at the orphanage when she met Harold. "He made this for me—the day I arrived in this old place." She pointed at where Jamie was standing. "I was standing right where you are now when he walked up to me and placed it around my neck. It was the first time in all my life I felt loved."

"But I thought this house used to be an old orphanage?" Jamie asked, confused.

"It was," Martha said with quivering lips. "Your dad and I were orphans. It's how we met."

No one knew this about Martha, not even Jamie. She had kept that part of her life a secret. Lucas and Trinity looked at each other and then walked over to their grandmother and hugged her. It was all they could think to do. Jamie's eyes filled with tears as she looked down at the photo. Now she knew why this photo seemed familiar when she had seen it earlier. It was her dad.

"I had no idea," Jamie said with a soft tone. "Why didn't you just tell me the truth?"

"I wanted to," Martha replied, "On many occasions. But after your dad died, as you got older, you began to resent me, and we grew distant. And you kept your distance. I only made it worse by trying to convince you I was a witch. You and your friends all laughed and called me crazy." Martha looked down sadly and hesitated. "Imagine if I had told you I was an orphan too. Not only would you not have believed me, but you wouldn't have wanted me, either. You were all I had left in this world. I couldn't lose you completely. So I kept it a secret."

Jamie's heart grew heavy with sadness, and she burst into tears—overwhelmed with guilt for the many wasted years that had passed. She walked over, sobbing uncontrollably, and fell into her mom's embrace. She felt like a kid once more in her arms. "I'm sorry!" she said, handing the picture back. "I'm so sorry! For everything!"

Martha took the picture and carefully placed it in her hair for safekeeping. She wiped Jamie's tears with one of her curls, hugged her, and kissed her on her head—but not before collecting and storing those tears in a small vial she'd pulled from her hair. *One never knows when genuine tears will be needed for mixing a potion.* She then gently lifted Jamie's chin and looked into her eyes. "Me too," she said. "Me too."

Bubbles walked over, trying to hide the fact that she was also crying (*weeping* more like it), and gave Martha and Jamie a firm hug. "Ma … ha … ha … haaaaaa," she bleated with a heave—which meant absolutely nothing in goat. She was just sad, and that's how she sounded when she cried, though she would never admit to crying. She was way too tough for that!

"OK, OK," Martha said, laughing, trying not to make a big deal out of the situation. She wiped her eyes. "Enough of that. Let's go home!"

"Mahahahah," Bubbles bleated, which meant, "Here. You'll need this." She handed Martha her broom.

"Thanks," Martha said, grabbing the broom. Bubbles nodded, still sniffling a bit. Then Martha cleared a circle and knelt down. She laid her broom on the floor and told everybody to join her. And so they did. One by one, they each got down on their knees.

Martha reached into her hair, pulled out her gloves, and slid them back on. She wasn't complete without her entire kooky ensemble. "OK," she said, giving them a dainty tug. "Everybody, place one hand on the broom and one hand on the floor."

They all did as Martha said while looking at each other nervously, but none were more nervous than Martha. Only a few bristles remained, and she was going to need them all for this to work properly—*there was no room for any mistakes.* It was her only shot at making it back safely to the correct timeline with her family, *along with her house. Here goes nothing,* she thought as she took another leap of faith—this time—on herself.

"Everybody close your eyes," she said. "And count to three."

Martha crossed every finger she could and even her toes and hoped for the best. For an added measure of good luck, she also crossed her eyes. After that, they all closed their eyes and counted to three.

"One ... two ... three!"

CHAPTER NINETEEN

KNOCK-KNOCK

As soon as everyone opened their eyes ... they were home!

It was unbelievable! Martha's plan had worked. They were all safely back in Texas, back on Martha's land, where it all began, and the timeline was correct too. Martha shoved her wonky broom into her hair without realizing it was like new and full of bristles once again. She jumped on the tips of her toes, dancing happily with no regard for how silly she looked. Martha reached back into her hair, pulled out the photo of Harold, and kissed it over and over. *Mwah. Mwah. Mwah.* After she had kissed it enough times, she returned it to the deepest, darkest hiding place within her hair, tucking it safely behind her curls so she would never part from it again.

Lucas ran to the window and looked outside to make sure they were home. Yep! They were back all right—excited and relieved that everything was back to normal. What a day!

And there was a bonus—Martha's house had been completely restored to the way it was before. Not a single thing was out of place.

Her magic, however, still wasn't fully charged. Even so, she felt whole once again.

Lucas and Trinity would have much to discuss after sharing the unwanted adventure of a lifetime. Their bond was now stronger than it had ever been before. Jamie was also able to patch things up with Martha. She learned a lot about her mom that morning and made peace with knowing she was a bona fide witch. This felt like a fresh start for all of them.

"What an adventure!" Lucas shouted with a smile from ear to ear.

"You can say that again!" Trinity agreed, joking that they should do it again sometime.

"I don't think so," Jamie said. "That was enough adventure for a lifetime." All she wanted now was to finally take a shower. Her body was exhausted, and her feet were black from how dirty they were—and she was somehow still covered in sand—and now soot!

On the plus side, though, traveling by bristle this time didn't affect her stomach one bit. In fact—it didn't feel like she'd traveled by bristle at all. *I must be getting used to this*, she thought.

"Where's Bubbles?" Lucas asked his grandmother.

"Yeah," Trinity said. "I don't see her anywhere."

"I dunno," Martha said, looking around, wondering the same thing.

"What if she didn't make it back?" Lucas asked, worried. "We should go look for her."

"No," Martha said calmly. "I'm sure she made it back safely. She'll turn up eventually. Chances are she transformed back into a goat." Martha made a funny face and a goat sound. "Mahahahaha!"

Lucas laughed.

"Don't worry," Martha assured him. "She's skittish as a goat. She's probably hiding somewhere outside. I'll check on her later."

But Martha was the one hiding; *she was hiding the truth.* She couldn't sense Bubbles's presence—*anywhere.*

And there was one other thing she was hiding that was even stranger.

Martha had no idea how they'd made their way back home!

Martha didn't tell the others. But it wasn't her magic that had brought them back safely, and she definitely wasn't responsible for her house being restored, either. She hadn't done any of it! In fact, she'd never even gotten the chance to pluck those last few bristles from her broom. Something else had brought them back— something much stronger—and much more powerful than Martha or her broom. But what? Martha couldn't figure it out. She had a bad feeling, though. It was unsettling. Her witch senses were tingling like crazy. But for the moment, there was nothing she could do. She was back home with her family, and that was all that mattered. Now, it was time to eat.

Going back in time over a thousand years, traveling across the world, battling a dragon, and saving an entire kingdom all in a single morning sure worked up an appetite. So, Martha planned a fantastic afternoon feast! Though she wasn't fully charged, she had plenty of magic to whip up her family's favorite foods. It was quite a spread, too—never-ending pizza for Lucas, lasagna stacked to the ceiling for Trinity, plus a giant jar of peanut butter and a spoon, and some of the best-tasting Texas barbecue ribs for her and Jamie. Their love for great barbecue was something they'd always had in common. And though Martha had no clue where Bubbles was, she honestly thought she'd turn up sooner or later. So she made her a tuna and cotton candy sandwich, which may seem strange to most, but it was Bubbles's absolute favorite. But Martha didn't need to use magic to conjure this stinky concoction. She prepared it the old-fashioned way—by using her own two hands. There was never a shortage of tuna cans and bagged cotton candy in this witch's pantry.

Martha loaded her table with so much food that it sagged in the middle. The table legs were bowed from all the weight and looked like they were about to snap in half. And she didn't stop there. She also used her magic for dessert. With what little room was left on the table, she filled it with a heaping pile of tasty pastries and delicious pies—*but no cake!* Martha had learned her lesson. However, she did have one other sweet addition she felt was a must-have for any gathering. She reached into her hair and pulled out a jar filled to the brim with Booger Blasters from Mr. Ferguson's shop, the Tasty Treat.

"Mmmm-mmmm," she said. They were her favorite. She especially liked the way they made her boogers taste. But she didn't pick her nose in front of anyone. She had more class than that. She waited until she was alone.

Everything looked scrumptious, and it smelled amazing. But there was still one thing missing—*coffee.* Martha hadn't had a single cup of coffee all day. For someone who owned a coffee shop, one day without coffee felt like a lifetime. So she reached back into her hair, pulled out a freshly brewed pot of Texas-style pecan-flavored coffee, and enjoyed many cups, back to back, like she was drinking liquid gold. Lucas and Trinity laughed. Watching Grandma dig things out of her hair never got old.

They all sat together as a family, sharing laughter and joy, and ate and ate until their bellies were stuffed and they could eat no more. But nobody ate the Booger Blasters except for Martha. She finished half the jar alone. Jamie did, however, let out a rather unexpected fiery belch that reached across the table and singed one of Martha's curls completely off. It was startling for a moment but nothing concerning. They all laughed while she patted out the flame.

Afterward, Jamie finally enjoyed the shower she deserved, and Lucas and Trinity took off together, recounting their unbelievable morning. Martha stayed in the kitchen. She still had one more thing she needed to do and waited until she was alone to do it.

Once Martha was certain no one else was around, she summoned Sparkly Martha one final time. But this time, she didn't summon her for help, and she didn't summon her from her nose. Instead, Martha simply called upon her, humbly requesting her appearance—so that Martha could do something Sparkly Martha wasn't expecting at all. But it was something Martha felt she should have done much sooner. Once Sparkly Martha magically appeared, Martha offered a sincere apology for her behavior earlier that morning and thanked her from the bottom of her heart for all that she did for her and her family. She even told her to kick up her sparkly feet and enjoy a cup of coffee—while *Martha* cleaned for once. For the first time ever, Sparkly Martha wasn't forced to do *anything.*

Then, Martha did something even more unexpected. She offered Sparkly Martha the freedom to be herself and promised never to summon her or take her for granted ever again. She only wanted her friendship and occasional assistance—but only if Sparkly Martha was inclined to do so. From now on, it was up to her. She was no longer Martha's helper. She was her partner and friend.

Sparkly Martha was now completely free and in charge of her own destiny. This was very exciting! Sparkly Martha had never before had any time for herself—to do the things *she* wanted to do. So this was the perfect opportunity for her to take a much-needed and well-deserved vacation. She accepted Martha's apology and thanked her with a giant sparkly hug. She nodded, "Goodbye for now," and then set off to see the world.

After Sparkly Martha went her own way, Martha slipped on her rubber farm boots, grabbed the tuna and cotton candy sandwich she had made, and went outside to search her property for Bubbles. She didn't know if she would find Bubbles the goat or Jezebel the human who *sounded* like a goat—or come up entirely empty-handed. But either way, Martha was determined to find her friend, *whichever* form she took. So she walked and searched—and walked and searched—and walked and searched. She walked and searched for hours, thoroughly checking every square inch of her land, whistling and calling out, "Bubbles? Bubbles?"

But Bubbles never answered.

No matter where she seemed to look, Bubbles was nowhere to be found. Finally, she had to reach into her hair and pull out a flashlight because it was getting dark outside. And it was a good thing this particular flashlight was waterproof—because Martha even dunked her head in her own pond to look underwater. Silly? Maybe. Foolish? Definitely. But she left no stone unturned. Unfortunately, Bubbles wasn't there either, only fish, fish, fish, and more fish.

Next, after wringing out all the filthy pond water from her hair, she gripped the flashlight with her teeth and climbed her magnificent oak tree *and all of her other trees* to look up high.

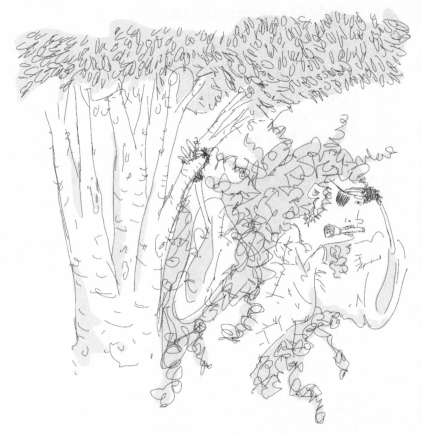

But still, there was no sign of Bubbles—only branches and leaves. She even managed to get on top of her house to search the roof and utilize the best view of her land possible. But again, Bubbles wasn't there, only shingles and crusty bird poop. She shined her flashlight, turning in a circle like a lighthouse, hoping Bubbles could see the light. But nothing. Martha didn't know what else to do. She sat on her roof for a while and waved the smelly sandwich around, hoping the fishy aroma would carry through the air and draw Bubbles out—but nothing. Nothing. Nothing. Nothing. Maybe Martha's fears were confirmed. Perhaps Bubbles hadn't made it back after all.

After climbing back down to the ground, Martha sadly returned inside after a thorough but failed search. She decided it would be best to wait and fully charge her magic before making her next move. Besides, she knew Bubbles was more than capable of taking care of herself. In the meantime, she would devise a few plans and then decide which one was best. And there was no better place to brainstorm than Martha's favorite spot in her entire house—her old blue recliner. So she moseyed over, planted her tired butt in her chair, and waited for the perfect plan to enter that big noggin of hers.

Later that evening, after the sun went down, when all was finally calm, there was an unexpected knock at the door.

Knock! Knock!

All the lights in the house began to flicker, and a hair-raising, freakishly frightening chill saturated the air—one only Martha could feel. Her witch senses were tingling like crazy, this time *off the chart.*

Then—another knock.

Knock! Knock!

Who could that be? she thought. She wasn't expecting any visitors. She sat up in her chair. Jamie was on the couch with her kids, finally wearing her own clothes and very relaxed after a long hot shower. Trinity was enjoying having internet service once again. She and Lucas were looking through her phone and posting all of the unbelievable pictures she had taken.

Jamie lifted her head. "Want me to get that, Ma?"

Martha didn't answer. She had a dreadful look of worry on her face.

"I'll get it!" Lucas shouted. He jumped off the couch and ran to the door. Before Martha could stop him, he opened it.

"Grandma!" he shouted with excitement. "It's Bubbles!"

But then—Lucas looked up with fright. Bubbles wasn't alone. Lucas slowly backed away from the door, pinching his nose while holding his breath. A foul, pungent, revolting odor punched its way through the house. The smell was bad enough to singe the hair off the backside of a fully-grown troll. It was unbearable! Jamie and Trinity also covered their noses.

"That's awful!" Jamie said. "What is it?"

"It wasn't me," Trinity snickered. But this was no laughing matter.

It smelled like …

Rot … dog vomit … and papaya!

"Cinnamon sticks!" Martha gasped. "A bad witch!" She sprung from her chair and raced to Lucas. "Go to your mom!" she commanded.

Lucas ran back to his mom.

Jamie stood in a panic. "What is it, Ma?" she asked a second time with concern.

Martha still didn't respond. Lucas and Trinity knew something was terribly wrong by the look on their grandmother's face and hid behind their mom.

Martha was right. There was definitely a bad witch present—but not just one.

There in the doorway stood none other than the master witch herself—Lady Bishop—with the entire Council at her back!

You see, the moment Martha and her family traveled back in time and lifted Jezebel's curse, the Council noticed—one witch in particular, *Ruby Redenbacher*. But the Council also sensed a great and powerful magic. So they sought Martha out—*and found her.* It was the Council who had truly been responsible for bringing Martha and her family back *and* restoring her house to the way it was. Now—they wanted a little something in return. They were there to claim what was owed to them.

Every member of the Council, including Lady Bishop, was cloaked in an old, worn, black-hooded robe. The stitching was torn at the seams, and the bottom was stained with a thick black goop. They all looked the same, identical from top to bottom, each blending with the night. Like statues, they stood still and quiet, not a single movement or peep.

But Lady Bishop stood out from the rest. *Her* robe was glowing with a magical spell, making her taller than the other witches, *much, much* taller.

She was a staggering nine feet tall!

The master witch had to bend over to fit through Martha's doorway. She seemed to float across the floor as she entered the house. Once inside, she had to stay hunched so her head wouldn't hit the ceiling. After staring for a while in silence, she held out her hands. In one hand, she held Bubbles, muzzled and leashed, and in the other, she held a special mason jar protected by a spell. Martha noticed that Sparkly Martha was trapped inside the jar. Lady Bishop clearly had cruel intentions.

Martha knew she had to do something to help. But before she could even react, Lady Bishop *attacked with magic.* She stomped her foot, rattling the entire house, and with only a tiny smidgen of magic from her little pinky toe, Jamie, Lucas, Trinity, and Martha were all frozen stiff. It was powerful magic! Struggle as they might, they couldn't move.

Lady Bishop slowly lowered her hood. As soon as she did, to everyone's surprise, she magically shrank down to her actual size, which was shockingly only four feet tall. Even her robe shrank in size and now just looked like a dingy used-up bathrobe. But don't let her size or appearance fool you. She may have been one of the oldest and *possibly* shortest witches alive, but she was still the most powerful *and* the most ruthless.

Lady Bishop was so corrupt with power that, over the years, she had warped into a short, chubby, beastly-looking woman with singed, ashy-white hair and rotten yellow teeth. Her flesh was dinosaur old and dry like petrified leather. Even the black boots she wore had warped, melting into her skin. And her magic was simply too much to contain. It *poured* out of her. A dreadful, grim, ghoulish-green fire blazed from her eyes and fingertips, and when she spoke, the words blazed from her mouth.

"I've been looking for you," Lady Bishop said with a wicked tongue and a mouthful of halitosis. Her voice was sharp, her tone direct. "I didn't know there was another witch out there with power like my own." Lady Bishop shook the Mason jar, taunting Martha.

Like in a game of poker, she was showing her hand, and Martha knew she couldn't beat it.

"You've been a busy little witch, haven't you?" Lady Bishop stated, raising the jar to her face. "This is quite the interesting helper you have." She shook the jar once more before hiding it in her robe.

"What is it you want with me?" Martha asked, struggling to speak against the magic.

But Lady Bishop didn't answer. "And my oh my," she said. "That cake you made? Now that was a wondrous work of art! I can't believe you pulled it off. How on earth were you able to find a dead cat that's been buried twice? I myself have never been able to get my hands on something that valuable. I always forget where I've buried them the first time around."

"What is it you want with me?" Martha asked a second time.

Still, Lady Bishop didn't answer. She stared up and down as if she was studying Martha and continued to rant. "Quite impressive if I do say so myself. Under any other circumstance, I do believe you and I could become great friends. Why, I'd even consider giving you a seat at the Council. I'd love to see the spells *you* bring to the table." She *yanked* on Bubbles's leash aggressively, and Bubbles yipped. "Just don't try anything foolish like this one," she added.

Then, she slowly walked around Martha, running her hand through her hair and curling the strands around her long, crooked, boney fingers—at one point even leaning in to get a whiff. *Snnnniff. Snnnniff.*

"How is it that you manage this glorious mess?" she asked, jokingly tossing her *own* head back and running her hand through the tiny bit of hair she had remaining. A couple of strands even fell out as she did so. "Such volume. Such luster. Oh, and you're welcome, by the way, for bringing you back from that godawful place *and* restoring your house. I even took the liberty of refilling your broom with more bristles. What you've done with your broom is neat, but you shouldn't tamper with tradition."

After it seemed like Lady Bishop had finally finished talking, she reached out her arm, extending it like a bridge, and out from under her sleeve—*came a rat.* With its beady red eyes and crinkled whiskers, the mangy rat scurried across her arm and leapt into Martha's hair, burrowing and tunneling about like it was wandering through a maze. Then, digging around, it found something.

As it crawled out of Martha's hair and onto her skin, she noticed that the rat had one of her magical lollipops between its two little sharp teeth—the same lollipops she used to transform naughty children into frogs. *This is it*, she thought, cringing each time the rat's cold paws touched her skin. This was her chance. If she could somehow get Lady Bishop to eat that lollipop, she could turn her into a frog and gain the upper hand.

But her plan would soon fail—because Lady Bishop was well aware of the magic contained in each lollipop, and she had every intention of eating it, regardless. She wasn't worried at all.

The rat went crawling back to Lady Bishop and whispered into her ear. Lady Bishop licked the lollipop with her long, slimy, snakelike tongue, enjoying the flavor while listening to her rat's squeaky whispers.

"I agree," she told the rat. "She is a strong one indeed."

However, Martha's magical lollipop had no effect on Lady Bishop. It merely tickled her taste buds.

"What is it you want with me?" Martha exploded a third and final time. She demanded to know!

Lady Bishop laughed. "Ha ha ha."

She tossed the lollipop to the floor and gave a sinister, wickedly-witchy stare—so chilling Martha felt it in her bones. But the short old witch wasn't staring at her.

Lady Bishop tapped her foot ever so gently against the floor, releasing her hold on Martha, allowing her to move—but only from the neck up.

"Not you," Lady Bishop said. "Silly old hag." She raised her arm and pointed, saying, "*You.*"

Martha turned her head.

Lady Bishop was pointing at—Jamie!

Without warning, the Council swarmed inside the house.

They all lowered their hoods and circled Jamie while holding hands, their witchy fingers locked tight. They chanted the same phrase over and over without stopping once and danced heinously, swaying their heads side to side as their eyes went pitch-black.

"Far away. To your new home. Come now, sister. Away we go. Far away. To your new home. Come now, sister. Away we go."

With each word they spoke, a black tar oozed from their mouths, dripping down their chin and onto the floor as they went 'round and 'round in a circle. The bottom of their robes dragged in the tar as they sploshed carelessly through the mucky substance with their bare feet.

Unable to move a single muscle, all Martha and her grandchildren could do was watch—sad, afraid, and helpless. There wasn't a thing they could do to save Jamie. They were outnumbered and out of magic.

Lady Bishop joined in as the Council chanted one last time. And together, with their voices combined, they completed a very powerful spell.

"Far away. To your new home. Come now, sister. Away we go!"

Lady Bishop and her wretched witches then magically vanished, taking Jamie with them—leaving behind no trace of where they had mysteriously come from or where they were going—only wicked laughter that echoed up, down, and all around before fading. Like thieves in the night, they witch-nabbed Jamie and then disappeared as quickly as they'd arrived. Once Lady Bishop was gone, her magical hold over Martha and her grandchildren was lifted, and they were able to move once again.

"They took Mom!" Lucas shouted, freaking out. "We have to go after them! We have to get her back!"

"We will," Martha assured him, trying to calm him down. "We will."

"*How?*" Trinity asked, also freaking out. "We don't even know where they went. They *literally* just disappeared into thin air, and not all *poof and pretty* like you do with your broom!"

Martha didn't answer. She paced back and forth for a moment, trying to gather her wits, muttering and mumbling to herself while switching her eye patch nervously from one eye to the other, back and forth multiple times.

"I think Grandma's cheese finally slid off her cracker," Trinity whispered to Lucas.

But then...

Martha stopped and pressed her lips, puckering them as if she was sucking on a very sour lemon, and squinted her eyes, *really squinting them*, until they couldn't be seen anymore—and a few seconds after—*she opened them wide and shook her finger high in the air.*

Lucas and Trinity knew exactly what that meant. *Grandma's getting an idea.* And boy, oh boy—what an idea it was!

"Well, Grandma—what do we do?" Lucas asked.

Now Martha answered.

"We conjure!"

ABOUT THE AUTHOR

Growing up, I had a BIG imagination! I enjoyed telling stories and drawing pictures, and I absolutely loved to make people laugh. That often got me into trouble, because I couldn't make everyone laugh. In the eighth grade, one of my teachers found me to be too distracting. She never laughed once. You can bet I was surprised when I walked into class one morning to find that my desk had been completely boxed in, using a large cardboard refrigerator box. Out of sight out of mind, I guess. Seems that teacher thought it would be a quick fix just to separate me from my "audience." True story. But it didn't work . . . I escaped!

Made in the USA
Coppell, TX
14 January 2024